The Animal Shelter

THE
ANIMAL SHELTER

Patricia Curtis

photographs by David Cupp

LODESTAR BOOKS   E. P. Dutton   New York

LIBRARY OF CONGRESS CATALOGING IN PUBLICATION DATA

Curtis, Patricia.
    The animal shelter.

    "Lodestar books."
    Bibliography: p.
    Includes index.

    Summary: Discusses the history and function of S.P.C.A.
and other humane shelters which provide temporary care for
stray, unwanted, lost, and abused animals in need of protection
from the ignorance, indifference, neglect, and cruelty
of human beings.
    1. Animals, Treatment of—Juvenile literature.
[1. Animals—Treatment—Societies, etc.
2. Pets]   I. Cupp, David, ill.   II. Title
HV4708.C87   1983   636.08′3   83-8908
ISBN 0-525-66783-0

Published in the United States by E. P. Dutton, Inc.,
2 Park Avenue, New York, N.Y. 10016

Published simultaneously in Canada by
Fitzhenry & Whiteside Limited, Toronto

Editor: Virginia Buckley   Designer: Riki Levinson

Printed in the U.S.A.   COBE   First Edition
10 9 8 7 6 5 4 3 2 1

This book is dedicated to Gretchen Scanlan, with gratitude, on behalf of all the many animals she sheltered with such compassion and good care.

Contents

Acknowledgments

FOR THE INSPIRATION FOR THIS BOOK, I am indebted to the thousands of dogs and cats I've seen in the many shelters I have visited. Their eyes, their voices, their often frantic attempts to communicate their plight to me motivated me to try my best to speak for them.

As for the people who gave me valuable information and advice, I especially wish to thank Phyllis Wright, Director of Animal Sheltering and Control, the Humane Society of the United States.

In addition, I gratefully acknowledge the cooperation and help of Robert D. Rohde of the Denver Dumb Friends League; John F. Kullberg, Joan Silaco, Sheryle Trainer, and Ursula Goetz of the ASPCA; Alice K. Gardan of the Women's SPCA of Pennsylvania; Judith Star of the American Humane Education Society; Estelle Wagner and Clark C. Martin of the Animal Rescue League of Western Pennsylvania; Kathy Bauch of the Anti-Cruelty Society; Arthur G. Slade of the Animal Rescue League of Boston; Carolyn G.

Bird of Red Acre Farm; Bill Garrett and Katey Breen of the Atlanta Humane Society; Sienna LaRene and David K. Wills of the Michigan Humane Society; Marge Wright of the Arizona Humane Society; John A. Hoyt, Frantz Dantzler, and Janet Frake of the Humane Society of the United States; Virginia Chipurnoi of the Humane Society of New York; and Dimitri Deharak of the Central Vermont Humane Society.

I'd also like to mention, with affection and gratitude: Jean Stewart, Jolene Marion, Hope Sawyer Buyukmihci, Henry Spira, the staff of the Pets Are Wonderful Council, and my editor, Virginia Buckley.

David Cupp and I greatly appreciate those humane organizations whose kind cooperation made it possible to take the photographs for this book: the Denver Dumb Friends League, the San Francisco SPCA, the California Marine Mammal Center, the ASPCA, the Humane Society of New York, and the Ryerss' Infirmary for Dumb Animals.

A dog that was once someone's pet finds himself confined in a cage at an animal shelter.

The Animal Shelter

THE DOOR WAS SHUT before the brown puppy realized he had been put in a cage. The woman who had placed him there gave him a pat on the head and a bowl of water and then left.

The young dog began to run back and forth against the bars, barking frantically, but although people occasionally walked by and spoke to him kindly, no one let him out. His yelps turned into howls and whines. He felt utterly abandoned and frightened, caged in this strange place. After several hours of trying to communicate his misery at the top of his voice, he was exhausted. So he sat in a corner and whimpered abjectly at everyone who passed.

How did this come about—what had this pup done to wind up in a cage at the SPCA? Who had brought him there? The events leading up to his plight had begun a few weeks earlier.

For some years, a boy and a girl had begged for a dog. As Christmas approached, they intensified their campaign.

1

"We'll walk him—we'll come home right after school and take him out," the thirteen-year-old boy promised.

"We'll feed him and give him baths," added his eleven-year-old sister. "We'll take complete care of him ourselves. Please, can't we have a dog?"

Their parents discussed the matter between themselves and finally agreed that their son and daughter were old enough to take care of a pet. "It will teach them responsibility," said the father.

They decided to surprise them with a puppy for Christmas, so on December 24, they went to the SPCA shelter.

"I'm sorry, but it's against our policy to let our pets be adopted right before Christmas," said Karen Hamilton, the director of the shelter. "We ask people to come back after the holidays."

"Why?" asked the surprised couple.

"We've learned over many years that pets often don't do well in a new home when there's so much excitement and activity going on. They become frightened and nervous, or overstimulated and sick. Some animals become irritable from too much handling," explained Mrs. Hamilton. "Also, family members are often too busy during the holidays to give proper care and attention to a pet. Now, if you'd like to come back after New Year's . . ."

But the man and woman didn't wait to hear the rest. They walked out and drove to the nearest pet shop, where the salesman was only too glad to sell them a puppy. Neither the man nor the woman knew anything about dogs, but they bought a cute, cuddly, very young brown pup and brought it home.

The children, of course, were thrilled. They named their pet Snoopy. All during Christmas vacation, they played with him, fed him, and took him for walks. They showed him off proudly to their friends. They took turns having him sleep in their bedrooms overnight and cleaned up after him with no complaints. Snoopy naturally enjoyed all the affection and attention.

Then vacation ended, and the boy and girl went back to school. The father was at work all day, and the mother had a part-time job, so Snoopy found himself alone for long hours for the first time in his life. He barked and howled. In his loneliness and frustration, he began to chew up things he found around the house—a sneaker, a sofa pillow, a rubber boot. He was too young to be able to control himself for long periods, so he made many puddles and piles. Then, when the family came home, he was scolded and spanked so much that he began to live in a state of continual confusion and anxiety. The people who had given him so much love and company now always seemed mad at him. Why?

As the days passed, Snoopy became so upset that he began to throw up his food and make more messes than ever. His world shrank as he was confined more and more to the kitchen. The children were busy with school, friends, and activities, and the novelty of having a dog began to wear off. Neither of the parents gave Snoopy any attention themselves or insisted that the boy and girl take proper care of him. They seemed to think it was Snoopy's job to "teach the children responsibility."

And so, one day when the mother returned from work and found that, again, neither of the children had come home after school to walk the puppy, her patience gave out. She called them into the kitchen.

"That does it!" she exclaimed as she stood in the doorway pointing to the puddles on the floor. "We get rid of that puppy tomorrow."

"Oh, Mom," wailed the boy. "I couldn't come right home to walk him. I had band practice."

"And I had to visit Shirley and take her homework to

her—she had a cold and wasn't in school today," said the girl. She shook her finger at the puppy who crouched, trembling, under the kitchen table. "Snoopy, you're a *bad dog*!" she scolded loudly. "Why couldn't you *wait?*"

The dog, of course, had no idea what he had done wrong. Even if he had understood, he couldn't have helped himself. He had been alone all day, shut in the kitchen, and when at last he had heard his family coming home, he had been both overjoyed and apprehensive. As usually happened, they had become angry at him instantly. He waited, shaking, for the punishment he knew would follow.

The next day, Saturday, the father put Snoopy in the car. The boy had already left to go ice skating, and the girl was still asleep, so neither of them even said good-bye to the dog they had wanted so badly.

When the man walked into the SPCA shelter carrying the brown puppy, Karen Hamilton happened to be at the front desk. She recognized him from the time, a few weeks earlier, when he and his wife had come in to adopt a pet. She was not especially surprised to see him.

"I see you did get a dog," she remarked.

"We bought him in a pet shop," the man said. "But he's not working out."

"What's wrong with him?" asked Mrs. Hamilton. She petted Snoopy, who looked fearful and bewildered but responded to her gratefully. "He seems like a nice puppy."

The man looked slightly embarrassed. "Look, there's nobody home all day," he said defensively. "He makes messes. The kids are too busy to walk him. He chews up things."

"We could have told you how to raise a puppy and how to avoid those problems," said Mrs. Hamilton. "But you wouldn't listen, and now you want to get rid of him." She spoke quite sharply.

"Also, my wife discovered she's allergic to dogs," said

This man, like Snoopy's owner, is trashing a pet.

the man triumphantly. He had just thought of this excuse.

Mrs. Hamilton had heard the "allergy" story too many times. "Oh, did your wife have a skin test?" she asked.

The man looked blank. Skin test? he asked himself. What's that? "Well, we're sure it's the dog she's allergic to," he mumbled.

A cat, unaware that her owner is abandoning her, doesn't struggle as she is surrendered to a shelter.

Mrs. Hamilton picked up Snoopy and walked away. The man left, feeling a little guilty, but by the time he arrived home, he had put the whole incident out of his mind. To him, the puppy was an object, a toy that had become more trouble than entertainment, and so he had discarded it, just as most people dispose of objects they no longer want.

Snoopy is not a real dog, and yet he is very real—there are millions of Snoopies. In any animal shelter in the United States, right now, there are puppies like Snoopy, and they are there for more or less the same reasons he was.

Karen Hamilton is a composite person—she is created from many real women who work in animal shelters. The shelter she manages is imaginary, but it is typical of an SPCA or humane society shelter in a medium-sized American city. Most communities have at least one animal shelter, whether it is called the SPCA (Society for the Prevention of Cruelty to Animals), the Humane Society, or some other name. The events that happen in the SPCA I have created take place in real shelters, in real life.

There are some two thousand animal shelters, thousands of people who work in them—and millions of animals living and dying in them. The dogs, cats, and people in this story are symbolic of the typical real animals that come into shelters and the typical real people who take care of them.

2
Thrown-Away Pets

WHILE KAREN HAMILTON was putting Snoopy in his cage, a woman came into the shelter carrying a large gray-and-white cat.

"I'd like you to find a home for our cat," she said to Bill, the young man at the front desk.

"Why?" he asked. "What's wrong with it?"

"There's nothing wrong with her, she's a perfectly good cat, but we're moving to California."

"Why can't you take her with you?" Bill queried.

"It would be too much trouble to drive out there with a cat. Besides, she's eight years old. Once we get there and settled, we'd rather get a brand-new cat," said the woman, handing over her pet. "Her name is Isadora. She's spayed," she added as she filled out the surrender form Bill gave her.

Isadora looked upset but she didn't struggle. Half an hour ago, she had been curled up in a patch of sunshine on her favorite rug when her owner had suddenly picked her up and carried her to the car. Now, what was this strange place?

8

A cat, thrown away by his owner as Isadora was, is comforted by a shelter staff member.

She looked after her mistress's departing back. *Where is she going? She has forgotten me!*

Just then Mrs. Hamilton returned to the front desk.

"Owners moving," commented Bill as he slipped a narrow plastic collar with a number on it around Isadora's neck.

"It's just too much trouble to take you, so they deserted you, didn't they, kitty." The SPCA often accepted pets discarded by people who were moving. Mrs. Hamilton stroked the cat, who responded immediately by arching her back and rubbing her head against the director's hand.

"The owner even spoke of getting a *new* cat after she's settled in California, as though she were trading in a used car or vacuum cleaner," Bill reported bitterly.

He carried Isadora down a hall and into the room where Snoopy was and put her in a cage. Like Snoopy, the gray-and-white cat had never been confined in a cage before. She began to pace, searching for an escape. "Mew," she said plaintively. "Mew! Mew!"

Bill got back to the front desk just as a young woman came in carrying a carton.

"I have some more kittens for you!" she exclaimed cheerfully. "They're adorable. Our cat must have had a handsome husband this time. My kids hated to give up this batch."

Bill sighed as he handed her a surrender form. He lifted the flap of the carton and looked in. Four flowerlike faces on little balls of fluff peered up at him. He made no comment.

"What's the matter?" the young woman asked him. "I thought I was doing you a favor by donating them to you. Don't you make money selling pets? You can charge a lot for these kittens. I bet a pet store would have bought them from us."

Kittens barely old enough to leave their mother face the strange world of an animal shelter.

"Our adoption fees don't even begin to meet the expenses of caring for our animals," Bill answered. "We have to put healthy pets to sleep nearly every day, because so many more are turned in to us than get adopted."

"Well, I'm sure you'll have no problem getting rid of these," smiled the young woman as she turned to leave.

"By the way, don't you think it would be a good idea to have your cat spayed so she won't keep on producing kittens?" asked Mrs. Hamilton, who had overheard the conversation.

"Oh, no!" exclaimed the kittens' former owner as she headed for the door. "It's so nice for the children to see the miracle of birth."

"If I hear that one more time . . ." muttered Bill. He glanced at the tiny animals. "These look younger than she said. Their eyes are still blue. I hope they're fully weaned." He picked up two of the kittens, then the third. "I'll name you Luke Skywalker and you Han Solo, and this female can be Princess Leia. And you"—he gathered up the smallest one, who had enormous ears—"you're Yoda, no doubt about it."

Mrs. Hamilton laughed. "Too bad there aren't five so you could name one E.T.," she commented. "Be sure and put them where Dr. Buckley can check them over as soon as she comes in."

Dr. Buckley was the veterinarian for the shelter. She examined each new animal to see if it was healthy. The SPCA offered only healthy animals for adoption, and it also was necessary to prevent contagious diseases from coming into the shelter from a new animal that might be sick. Every new dog and cat was put in the room where Snoopy and Isadora were, separate from the rest of the animals, until the condition of its health could be established.

A batch of unwanted puppies is received at a shelter.

When Bill returned to the front desk, a woman with a large black dog on a leash was already speaking to Karen Hamilton.

"Yes, we've had her for ten years—we got her for the children when they were young," she said. "But the last child is off at college now, and my husband and I don't want to be tied down to such a responsibility. We'd like you to place Kate with someone else. She's perfectly healthy and has a gentle disposition."

The Labrador retriever sat patiently at the woman's feet, looking around.

"I have to tell you frankly, the chances of anyone wanting to adopt a ten-year-old dog are very slim," Mrs. Hamilton said. "We'll probably have to put your dog to sleep. I think you should realize that."

"Oh, dear," said the woman. "She's such a nice dog. Can't you put an ad in the paper for her or something? The kids would be upset if they thought she'd been destroyed."

"Couldn't you have put an ad in the paper yourself and tried to find a home for her? We have over seventy dogs here now, and ideally we have room for only about sixty without crowding." Mrs. Hamilton was trying not to show her anger. "People who adopt usually want younger dogs or puppies. If you aren't willing to keep her, or to find another home for her yourself, we will do the best we can, but we can't work miracles. Placing a dog her age in an adoptive home would be a miracle."

Kate began to sense that she was the object of the discussion between her owner and this strange woman. They kept looking at her. What was going on? She got the feeling that something was about to happen that would affect her, and that it wasn't good.

Her owner tapped her fingers on the counter. "Well, my husband and I have already made plans for a long trip," she said, looking guilty but determined. "We just can't keep Kate. It's too much trouble for us to have a dog at this point in our lives." Kate looked at her owner uncertainly, then licked her hand.

The woman quickly signed the surrender form and rushed out.

Mrs. Hamilton and Bill didn't say a word to each other. They didn't have to—each of them knew what the other was thinking. Kate's owner had simply done what most of us in the United States are accustomed to doing: trashing what we no longer want. This point is stressed by Dr. Alice De Groot, a veterinarian involved in public education on the care of animals: We simply throw away what is no longer desirable or convenient—even if it is a living, thinking, feeling creature.

Kate began to tremble as Mrs. Hamilton picked up the leash and led her back to the new arrivals room. Kate went into her cage without hesitation, walked to the back, and lay down with her face to the wall. Mrs. Hamilton spoke to her and petted her, trying to reassure her, but Kate paid no attention. She knew what had happened.

The next dog that was brought into the shelter didn't come from a home and probably hadn't had one in a long time, if ever. A boy was pulling it by a rope around its neck, but the animal was badly frightened. It was a black-and-brown, extremely dirty, medium-sized dog of no particular breed. It had a small, ugly-looking sore on its back, and though it was skin and bones, it had a potbelly.

"I found him," explained the teenager. "He was trying to eat garbage in a vacant lot. I felt sorry for him. It took me two hours to catch him—I brought him some food, and while he was eating I slipped the rope over his head. Could you take him? I know my mother would never let me bring him home."

"You did the right thing," Bill told the boy. "He would

have starved to death, died of disease, or been killed by a car. That's what happens to almost all homeless animals. We'll take care of him—thanks for bringing him in." Bill crouched down and took the rope from the boy. "Here, fellow, don't be afraid," he said to the dog, who shied away.

Mrs. Hamilton filled out a card to be attached to the dog's cage door. "We'll call you Tim because you're so timid," she said to the animal.

Bill coaxed Tim down the hall to the special section where sick or injured animals were kept temporarily until seen by the veterinarian. After he got the dog into a cage, he put a bowl of water and some chow in with him. Tim cowered at the back of the cage, but when Bill left, he crept forward and drank and ate eagerly.

Tim wasn't the only stray brought into the shelter that day. David, one of the animal control officers, drove the shelter's van into the driveway and removed a cat carrier from the back. A large, dirty, yellow-striped cat glared out.

"Wow, did I have a time getting this one," announced David to Mrs. Hamilton. "Some people apparently had moved away and left him locked in an empty house. He had climbed up the chimney trying to get out."

David set the carrier down, and the animal began to scratch at the top and sides. "He was perched on a narrow projection about halfway up the chimney, unable to climb up further and afraid to back down, I guess. Neighbors heard him crying and complained, said he'd been there several days. I had to get him from the roof."

A noose on the end of a long pole is often used to capture stray animals. The noose is slipped over an animal's neck and then tightened like a collar; the pole is then used to draw (or drag) the animal along. Called a come-along, this is used by many animal control officers. However, David always avoided using a come-along whenever possible, because it

A new arrival wonders what all those cats are doing here, while shelter staff members wonder where to put him.

often frightens the animal. Besides, if he had tried to pull the cat out of the chimney with one, he might have strangled it, so he had used a little ingenuity: He had put some fish in the bottom of a burlap bag and lowered it down to the cat. The hungry animal, smelling the fish, had reached for the bag, and as soon as its front claws were sunk in the burlap, David had carefully and slowly raised the bag with the cat clinging to it.

"That was good work, David," said Mrs. Hamilton, looking in at the cat. "Do you think he's hurt?"

"Not the way he put up a fight when we grabbed him on the roof. He's just scared stiff and probably half-starved. He wolfed down the fish in the carrier on the way here, growling as he ate," said the animal control officer.

When the yellow cat was maneuvered into a cage, he flattened himself against the back and hissed and snarled. He was even too upset to eat and drink. At this point, he didn't trust anyone. His people had gone away and left him shut up in the house without food or water. He had waited and waited, and called in vain. Finally, when hunger pains became too severe, he had made his bid for freedom. He could see a little of the sky at the top of the chimney and had scrambled and clambered toward it, but he found he couldn't get all the way to the top and could no longer see the hearth below. He had no idea how long he had clung there. He had mewed desperately, becoming weaker by the hour.

Then he had heard someone above him, and food had been lowered. But when he tried to get at it, he couldn't open the bag, and he had been pulled up through space, clinging for his life. Suddenly he had found himself in daylight, but before he could run, someone had grabbed him and popped him in a box. Now here he was shut in a cage. He was rigid with fear. What was going to happen next?

3

A Case of Cruelty

"THIS CALL'S FOR YOU, JANE," said Bill, handing a slip of paper to the shelter's investigator. "A report on a cruelty case."

The young woman glanced at the address. "That's out at the south end of town," she said. "See you later." She put on the jacket and cap of her uniform and headed for the station wagon.

Someone had telephoned the SPCA to say that a dog chained to a doghouse seemed to be dead or dying. Normally, the dog could be seen walking back and forth on its chain or pawing at its food bowl, a neighbor reported, but now the animal was lying on the ground in front of the doghouse, not moving, and had been in that position for several hours, despite the freezing temperature.

As all shelter workers know, once in a while somebody may report a case of cruelty or neglect of an animal that turns out to be a false alarm—the person reporting may have made an honest mistake. Or someone may be having a feud with a neighbor, or be annoyed with his pet, and call the SPCA just to harass him. But it is a humane investigator's job to follow up all reports.

Jane found the address and rang the bell. When no one came to the door, she walked around to the back. There was the dog, lying on the frozen ground. Jane felt her pulse, and as she did so, the dog opened her eyes and tried to lift her head, but was too weak to move.

"What are you doing to my dog?" a voice asked, and Jane looked up to see a burly red-faced man walking toward her.

"I'm from the SPCA," said Jane. "We received a report about your dog. How long has she been lying here like this?"

"Only a few minutes," lied the man. "Why? What busybody reported that there was anything wrong with her?"

"She is almost frozen, and she looks sick," replied Jane. "And she's greatly underweight. Look at that food bowl—the food is rotten and frozen. This doghouse is no protection from the cold—it's falling apart. I'm going to have to take this dog to the shelter."

"You can't take my dog!" exclaimed the man, getting angrier.

"I'll make a deal with you," the humane officer said, straightening up and speaking calmly to the belligerent man. "Why don't you give her to us and let us take care of her. That way the treatment and care won't cost you anything. Otherwise, I'll have to take the dog into protective custody and give you a summons. You can't treat a dog this way—it's cruel."

"There ain't a court in the world that would declare me guilty," said the man stubbornly. "This mutt is my property, and I have a right to treat her any way I please."

"No, you don't. There are laws that protect animals, even

when they are someone's property," Jane told him. When the man began to argue further, she wrote out a summons and handed it to him. He threw it on the ground.

Jane lifted the dog and started toward the station wagon. The man watched her go, muttering insults, but he made no move to stop her. From experience, SPCAs have learned that women make better humane investigators than men. They are less threatening and intimidating to people, and are usually able to win their cooperation. If Jane had felt she was in any danger, she would have left the scene immediately and handled the case with help. But she was certain the man would do nothing, and in fact, all he did was complain and curse.

When Jane entered the shelter's clinic carrying the dog in a blanket, Dr. Buckley had arrived and was putting on her white coat. She looked at the animal and her face immediately showed concern. As Jane put the dog on the table, the animal gave a feeble, rasping cough. A heavy discharge had run from her eyes and mouth onto the blanket, and her breathing was shallow.

"Pulse very weak," said Dr. Buckley. She examined the dog. In a few minutes, she shook her head and put her stethoscope in her pocket.

"This dog is so far gone, I'm sure she won't make it," she said. "And she must be suffering." She turned to Karen Hamilton, who had come to the clinic when she heard Jane had returned. "It might be best to euthanize her."

Mrs. Hamilton spoke soothingly to the dog and petted her, but the animal was unconscious now. She nodded to Dr. Buckley. The veterinarian took a hypodermic needle from her medicine cabinet and filled it with sodium pentobarbital, an anesthetic that, when given in a large dose, will kill an animal painlessly and quickly. In a few seconds, the sick, starved, and frozen animal was beyond her pain.

A sick dog, homeless and alone in a vacant lot, is rescued by an animal control officer.

"Chained to a doghouse!" exclaimed Mrs. Hamilton. "That should be against the law in any kind of weather. It's a horrible way for a dog to live." As many years as she had been involved in work with animals, she was still amazed at the results that she saw of people's cruelty.

By midafternoon, Dr. Buckley had examined all the new arrivals at the shelter. Snoopy was given a clean bill of health and moved to a kennel room where there were other puppies in cages on all sides of him. He seemed to cheer up a bit when he could see the others.

Isadora submitted quietly to being examined and was also found to be healthy. She was carried to the cat room, where cages filled with cats of all sizes and colors lined the aisles. Some were together in large cages, some were by themselves. Isadora crouched in the front of her cage and looked out, as if she were still expecting her owner.

An anxious dog pleads to be rescued from a shelter.

Kate was not interested in anyone or anything. She had refused food and acted as if she had lost her will to live.

"This dog is deeply depressed," said Dr. Buckley to Mrs. Hamilton as they stood looking with sympathy at the totally despondent Labrador retriever. In some big-city shelters, Kate would have been euthanized immediately. Most people prefer to speak of "putting an animal to sleep," but *euthanize* is the correct word for deliberately and painlessly killing a living creature.

When a severely injured or very sick animal is brought into a shelter, it is almost always euthanized immediately. Most shelters have so many animals continually coming in that they can't afford to give prolonged and costly treatment and care to any one, especially one whose survival chances are slim.

Animals are often euthanized for other reasons, too. Old age is one factor. A cat over two years of age or a dog over three or four is considered old and may be euthanized simply because its chances of being adopted are not very good. People coming to adopt usually want kittens or young dogs. The future looked very uncertain for eight-year-old Isadora and ten-year-old Kate.

"But they would make nice pets," said Mrs. Hamilton. "We'll keep them as long as we can. Someone may come in soon who'll want an older pet."

The four kittens seemed quite content and were not crying for their mother. They had eaten without difficulty.

"They're all okay except this little one here," announced Dr. Buckley, picking up Yoda. "He needs to grow a little before he can be put up for adoption. Is there anyone who could take him home and give him extra feedings, keep him warm, and watch him for maybe a week?"

Jody, a teenage volunteer at the shelter, spoke up. "I'll take him." She held the tiny creature in her cupped hands. Jody was a freshman at a community college. "I'm on my semester break," she said to Dr. Buckley. "I don't have classes again till next week, so I can give him lots of special attention."

Dr. Buckley had her assistant hold Tim while she examined the sore on his back. Fortunately, all it needed in the way of medical treatment was first aid.

"You know, I think this is a burn that has become infected. Look—there are recent scars of similar lesions." She looked through the fur on the dog's back. "I wonder if he could have been caught in a shower of sparks in a fire. Or do you suppose somebody gave him the cigarette treatment?" She and Mrs. Hamilton exchanged looks. The torment of animals is not uncommon anywhere in the world. And apparently someone, or several people, in certain areas of the city was capturing stray animals and torturing them with lighted cigarettes, for a number of them had been brought to the shelter in recent weeks with deep, tiny, round burns.

Tim also looked as if he had worms, judging by his thin condition, dull coat, and round belly. Dr. Buckley ordered stool specimens to be taken so she could identify the internal parasites and give him the correct medicine.

Then she looked at the scowling yellow cat that David had rescued from the chimney. In making out an identification card for his cage, a shelter worker had named him Tiger. Both Dr. Buckley and Mrs. Hamilton were concerned about his chances. Obviously, a cat who was that unfriendly could never be offered for adoption, and the shelter was full of cats with good dispositions who needed homes.

Nevertheless, his background was unknown. There was one possibility in a million that somewhere there was a person who had owned him and would come looking for him. Tiger would be kept for at least three days, no matter how unhappy and disagreeable he was.

Unless a lost or stray animal is badly injured or ill, a shelter will keep it in order to give an owner the chance to come and claim it. Some shelters keep animals for only three days, others for up to a week, depending on their regulations, the condition of the pet, and whether or not the shelter is overcrowded.

There was also the chance that when Tiger recovered from his fear and shock, he might calm down and become friendly. Some dogs and cats that snarl and growl at people in shelters are actually pets who are normally gentle but who are hysterical with fear and anxiety over being abandoned or lost from their homes and owners.

And so, in one day, the SPCA shelter had acquired nine new animals. What did the future hold for Snoopy, Isadora, Kate, Tim, Tiger, and the kittens?

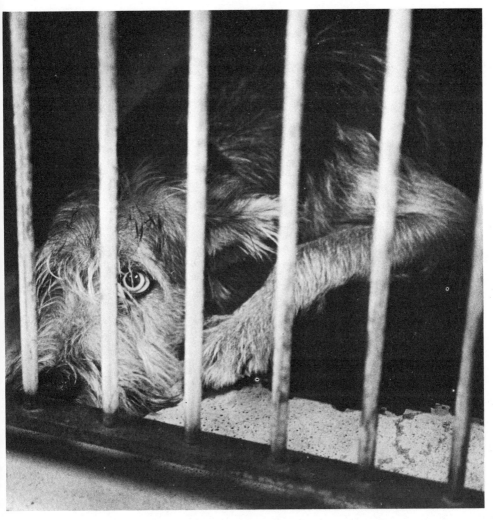

Time passes slowly for a lost and frightened dog. Will his owner miss him and come looking for him?

In order to consider the possibilities for their future, it's useful to look at the real past, to see how and why animal shelters were created. The story of humane shelters, which follows here in the next two chapters, is not symbolic but factual. The founders really lived, and the early events really happened.

Early
Humane Societies

IT WAS FOUR O'CLOCK on a cool spring afternoon in 1865 in New York City. Along the waterfront on the East River, men and boys were lined up waiting for the show. About three hundred dogs were tied up nearby, some barking and lunging at their chains trying to escape, some trembling with fear and looking anxiously about. These were stray dogs that had been rounded up by the city dogcatchers during the day.

Soon the poundmaster came along and pointed at random to a dozen or so dogs. He and the dogcatchers threw them quickly into a large crate and sealed the lid. The crate was attached to the arm of a crane that picked it up and swung it out over the river. As the dogs yelped and clambered over one another, the crate was lowered into the water and left there for some minutes. Then it was raised, carrying a sodden mass of drowned dogs.

"Hooray!" cheered the spectators gleefully.

An old print depicts the drowning of strays at the New York City dog pound. *Courtesy of Massachusetts SPCA*

But wait——a few animals in the crate could be seen feebly struggling, choking and gasping, trying to get their breath.

"Douse 'em again," yelled the men along the dock. Down into the water again went the crate. This time when it was raised, there was no movement among the soggy forms. The people watching cheered louder, enjoying the sight.

Again and again, the crate was filled with helpless dogs and lowered into the river. At last, all the wet, dead dogs were loaded onto a wagon and carted away. The show was over for the day, but it would be repeated the next day, and every day. This was the way the city of New York handled stray dogs in the 1860s. Some people enjoyed the sight; others simply went along with it; some preferred to ignore it as though it didn't happen. A few felt sorry for the animals.

A commonplace nineteenth-century scene: men brutally beating a horse that's trying to pull a heavy wagon from the mud, while bystanders look on unconcerned. *Picture Collection, Branch Libraries, the New York Public Library*

In other cities of the United States, more direct methods were used to rid the streets of stray dogs. Poundmasters simply chained up the animals and clubbed them to death.

Dogs that lived with their owners were often not much better off. People routinely starved, neglected, beat, or otherwise mistreated their dogs, and few gave it a second thought. As for other animals, it was a common sight to see drivers whipping horses as thin as skeletons hitched to heavy loads. When they staggered or fell, they were only beaten harder. And the less said the better about the treatment of cats, for in addition to being small and relatively defenseless, cats were surrounded by superstition. Ignorant people associated them with witches, the devil, and other such nonsense and persecuted them savagely.

Monstrous cruelty to animals of all kinds was the norm.

There lived at the time a wealthy New Yorker named Henry Bergh, who in all likelihood had witnessed the drownings of dogs in the East River. But he had apparently never thought to protest.

Bergh was already a middle-aged man when he experienced a profound change in his life, one that was to affect the lives of many people—and probably millions of animals. He was serving as a diplomat in Saint Petersburg, Russia, when he became horrified at the cruelty with which cart and carriage horses were treated. On returning to his native country, Bergh saw that the plight of horses here was just as bad. He vowed to devote his life to helping them.

Bergh realized he had a difficult job ahead, for in order to help animals, it would be necessary to change people's attitudes—which is not an easy task. Nevertheless, he threw himself into the work of reform with the zeal of a true crusader. First he gathered together a group of his friends who he felt would be sympathetic.

"I think two things are urgently needed at once," he said to them. "First, a law that will give animals some legal protection against cruel treatment. And second, there must be an organization that will not only see that the law is enforced but will also work to educate and influence the public, so that people will begin to recognize the cruelty all around us and stop participating in it."

Fortunately, there were enough sensitive New Yorkers who agreed with him. Bergh wrote a Declaration of the

Rights of Animals and was able to collect enough signatures on it to persuade the state legislators in Albany, the capital, that the people of New York felt that a strong anticruelty law for animal protection was needed. At the same time, he set about organizing a society of people who would be willing to help enforce the anticruelty law and urge the public to treat animals more kindly.

Henry Bergh was a hard man to ignore. He was six feet tall, wore a shiny, black top hat, and carried a fancy cane. He made fiery speeches and had an air of authority. He also had determination, courage, and energy.

In April 1866, he achieved his first two goals. An anticruelty law was passed that gave some protection to animals in New York State. And the American Society for the Prevention of Cruelty to Animals (ASPCA) was chartered, becoming the first humane organization in the United States. The ASPCA had the power to enforce the anticruelty law within the state of New York.

Bergh was a tireless and busy man. He seemed to be everywhere at once around the city, interfering with people who were mistreating animals, getting some arrested on cruelty charges, testifying in court against animal abusers.

The main form of transportation in the city in those days was by streetcars drawn by teams of horses. The horses often had to pull overloaded cars in blazing heat, or through streets slick with ice that caused them to fall and break their legs. Often the animals found themselves chest-high in snowdrifts or ankle-deep in mud, and when they fell, they were usually beaten by the drivers.

Then Henry Bergh might appear out of nowhere. "Stop beating those horses!" he would bellow. By sheer force of personality, he could usually persuade the drivers to make the people get out of the streetcars while he led the poor beasts out of their predicament. Bergh could also convince

The driver of this emaciated horse hitched to the overloaded wagon is in trouble; Henry Bergh (*fourth from left*) is having him arrested for cruelty. *Picture Collection, Branch Libraries, the New York Public Library*

the drivers that if they whipped the horses again, he would have them arrested.

Animals weren't the only ones who were mistreated in those days. Children were often abused by their parents or were hired out as drudges to live with and work for people who starved and whipped them freely. Sometimes parents or employers sent ragged children out in all kinds of weather to beg.

Abandoned children lived in the streets, eating garbage, begging for food, perhaps stealing in order to survive. There was no organization to protect children or shelter them.

But just as there were some men and women who wanted to put a stop to violence against animals, there were many who were strongly opposed to cruelty to children. Some of these people sought legal ways to bring children under the protection of the same law that Henry Bergh had designed to prevent cruelty to animals.

There was a famous court case in 1874 involving a child named Mary Ellen, who lived as a drudge with a woman who treated her brutally, starving and beating and overworking her. The plight of Mary Ellen was brought to the attention of Henry Bergh. At his instigation, a case was filed against Mary Ellen's employer, and the woman was ordered into court. The trial that followed was a significant one for children.

The room was filled with spectators when the judge called the court to order. Then a door opened and the little girl was carried in, wrapped in a horse blanket. The prosecutor laid her at the feet of the judge, who was so horrified at her condition that he turned his face away. People in the courtroom fell silent. Some were so moved they began to weep.

Then Henry Bergh spoke up: "If there is no justice for this child as a human being, she shall at least have the rights of the dog in the street. She shall not be abused!"

The woman who had mistreated Mary Ellen was sent to jail. This case marked an important moment in the history of all creatures who cannot defend themselves.

Soon after that, the New York Society for the Prevention of Cruelty to Children was formed. It used the offices of the ASPCA for its headquarters, and Henry Bergh agreed to serve as vice president.

Meanwhile, however, Bergh was traveling extensively around the United States, carrying his message. He made speeches, urging people to form societies like the ASPCA and take action in their own communities, cities, and states to protect animals from abuse. His words did not go un-heeded, for he found many others who were sick of the atrocities against animals that they saw all around them.

In some cities, active humane organizations were already forming. In 1868, a group of leading Philadelphians, led by a Colonel M. Richards Muckle, formed the Pennsylvania Society for the Prevention of Cruelty to Animals, the second humane society in the United States. That same year, across the continent, a banker named James Sloan Hutchinson founded the San Francisco SPCA. Both of these organizations are still very active.

And in the frontier town of Portland, Oregon, a group of businessmen, aroused by Thomas Lamb Eliot, a Unitarian minister, formed an organization to promote the humane treatment of animals "and all living things." It became the Oregon Humane Society and SPCA, and is still in existence. During its early years, it extended protection to abused children, orphans, prisoners, and the poor, as well as to animals.

Also in 1868, a well-to-do Boston woman named Mrs. William Appleton applied to incorporate a Massachusetts SPCA. Boston was just as bad as other communities in terms of common, everyday, hideous cruelty to animals. And most Bostonians ignored it.

Mrs. Appleton, encouraged by correspondence with Henry Bergh, had gathered a group of compassionate people around her to join the new Massachusetts SPCA when, by coincidence, something happened that advanced the cause of animals by a giant step.

A successful Boston lawyer named George Angell had been similarly appalled by the widespread mistreatment of animals. One day, when two horses were driven to death in a race, Angell wrote a letter that was published in a Boston newspaper urging everybody who was against such cruelty to get in touch with him, because he wanted to form an organization to try to prevent it. One person who immediately contacted him was Mrs. Appleton. Angell not only joined her group but accepted its leadership.

George Angell was much like Henry Bergh in his zeal to help animals and in his ability to get things done. Like Bergh, he felt the first order of business was to get an animal protection law passed and to obtain for the Massachusetts SPCA the power to enforce it. Angell, however, had an especially strong belief in humane education, particularly of children. He believed that people could be taught to be kind, and that if they understood the needs and feelings of animals, they would treat them with compassion, sympathy, and consideration.

"It's important to prosecute people who abuse animals and to arouse the conscience of the public against cruelty to them," he said. "But our children offer the strongest hope for change. It is with them that our best efforts must lie."

In his enthusiasm, he urged teachers to teach humane education in their classrooms. He also formed children's clubs to promote kindness to animals and conducted essay contests on this theme in Sunday school classes. Eventually, in 1899, he formed the American Humane Education Society, which is still active not just in Massachusetts but throughout the country. Today, there is also another such organization, the National Association for the Advancement of Humane Education, a branch of the Humane Society of the United States.

Angell also started a monthly magazine called *Our Dumb Animals* to spread humane education. In it, Americans first read a remarkable story about a horse that touched their minds and hearts and called their attention to the plight of horses in the same way that another book, *Uncle Tom's Cabin,* aroused people to the injustices of slavery. The story immediately became a best-seller, and its fame endures even today among children of many countries. Who has not read or at least heard of *Black Beauty?*

All over the United States, compassionate people were founding humane organizations to press for greatly needed reforms in the treatment of animals, especially horses. The SPCAs and humane societies did succeed in getting anti-cruelty laws passed and worked hard to enforce them; they persistently taught kindness to animals; they were doing much good. However, there was still no such thing as an animal shelter.

5

Reformers and Defenders

DESPITE THE FOUNDING of many humane societies across the United States in the late nineteenth century, life did not improve for animals overnight. Stray dogs were still routinely rounded up by dogcatchers, brought to the city pounds, and put to violent deaths. Thoughtless people who tired of their pets simply abandoned them in the streets, and sooner or later these animals died of starvation, disease, or torture, or fell into the brutal hands of the dogcatchers. There were no places where people could reclaim lost pets, adopt new ones, or where strays were sheltered or humanely killed.

In Philadelphia, a group of women were to change that and greatly influence the course of the humane movement.

The men on the governing board of the Pennsylvania SPCA had stated from the beginning that they welcomed ladies to assist them in their benevolent work. Although some of the founders were women, they served only in the Women's Branch of the organization. They were not allowed

to be members of the board of directors or to make decisions about the policies of the organization. Also, perhaps
the members of the Women's Branch were not favorably im-
pressed with the way the men were running the SPCA.

One outspoken founder named Caroline Earle White
raised an objection. "We women are doing most of the fund
raising, but we don't have any say in how the money we raise
is spent," she pointed out. "I think we should form our own
organization and elect our own board of directors."

The women agreed with her. And in 1870, they got a separate charter and became an independent society, the
Women's Pennsylvania SPCA, with a board composed en-
tirely of women.

Mrs. White and her band of active women didn't waste
time. One thing that especially concerned them was the city
dog pound. It was the custom of the dogcatchers to lasso
stray dogs, most of which were in a pitiful state of starvation
or disease. The wretched animals were often choked to death
by the lasso and, if they survived that, they were then
brought to the pound and beaten to death.

The Women's Pennsylvania SPCA immediately applied
to the city for the contract to take over the job of catching
stray dogs and disposing of them. They said it should be
done humanely. There was considerable opposition and ridicule from members of the city government, the press, and
the public. Who, they sneered, could seriously care about
stray animals? People today who defend animals are sometimes scoffed at and accused of being silly and sentimental.
The members of the Women's Pennsylvania SPCA and the
other humanitarians in those days had to endure a lot worse.

Nevertheless, thanks to the help of a sympathetic mayor,
the women were awarded the dogcatching contract and given
land on which to build a new pound. They immediately in-
structed the dogcatchers they employed to use nets instead

of lassos to capture stray dogs. And they raised the money to build a new, clean, comfortable pound, where the dogs were well treated. Those that had to be disposed of were killed by gas instead of clubbing. It opened in 1872, and the women called it the City Pound and Dog Shelter.

The addition of the word *shelter* to the name of the pound represented a meaningful change in attitude about the responsibility of people toward stray animals. In fact, two years later, one member of the Women's Pennsylvania SPCA, Elizabeth Morris, took this concept one step further and set up a place called the City Depot, where sick or injured dogs *and cats* were brought and either painlessly put to death or kept until they could be taken to the main pound and put up for adoption. Citizens of Philadelphia were encouraged to use the depot as a place to bring suffering animals that they found or to turn in their own pets that were incurably ill, injured, or no longer wanted.

So the women had established not only a decent pound that was also a shelter, but in addition they had created an animal shelter that was separate from the pound.

Their example of *sheltering,* and their use of a humane method of euthanasia, were important steps in helping the vast numbers of homeless and abandoned dogs and cats that roamed the streets of America, for soon other SPCAs were following suit. In April 1872, an issue of *Our Dumb Animals* carried a progress report of the Massachusetts SPCA's work over the preceding year. One item reads:

Following the example of London and Philadelphia, our Society have voted to establish a home for lost and disabled animals, a most merciful undertaking. The plan is to restore lost animals to their owners, find good homes for others which are valuable, and to mercifully kill by carbonic acid gas and chloroform such as are worthless.

This report did not explain what was meant by *valuable* or *worthless*. Perhaps by *valuable*, the writer meant healthy animals that were suitable for adoption. At any rate, in a report of the organization's work of the following year, a short note reads: "An Animals' Home has been established."

Caroline Earle White was a strong, no-nonsense woman who didn't hesitate to battle against many forms of cruelty to animals. The old pound had routinely supplied stray dogs to doctors for vivisection—medical experimentation on fully conscious living animals. The dogs were strapped to operating tables, cut open for research (without any anesthetic), and then left to die, often slowly, on the tables. The women refused to turn over any more dogs to the medical schools; they said the purpose of the pound was to give shelter and dispense mercy to animals, not to hand them over to further suffering. The doctors took the women to court, saying that they needed the animals for teaching and research, but the women remained firm and won their case.

Henry Bergh also opposed vivisection. George Angell did not get involved with the issue.

Mrs. White and her group directed many of their efforts at helping the city's workhorses. The streetcar companies of Philadelphia, like those in New York, made no allowances for the horses in severely cold or hot weather. They often sent cars out in violent snowstorms with only two horses hitched to them or forced the animals to pull overloaded cars in sweltering heat. It was not unusual for a horse simply to drop dead from exhaustion while still in harness. The Women's Pennsylvania SPCA worked hard to stop these inhumane practices.

Some years later, this group of compassionate and energetic women opened a greatly needed, free veterinary clinic, the first of its kind in the United States. It was named the Caroline Earle White Dispensary.

Courtesy of Women's SPCA of Pennsylvania

Early humane society ambulances.

Courtesy of Animal Rescue League of Boston

Courtesy of Bide-A-Wee Home Association

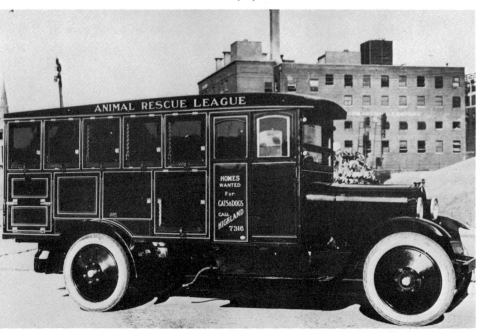

Courtesy of Animal Rescue League of Western Pennsylvania

The concerns of the women extended well beyond the animals of Philadelphia. Caroline White went to Washington to urge the passage of a national law to protect cattle. At that time, cattle were shipped across the country from the ranches to the slaughterhouses under grossly inhumane conditions: They were jammed into railroad cars and suffered unbelievably. Those that fell were trampled by the others. The journeys of the cattle cars took many days, during which the animals were given no food or water.

Congress did listen to Mrs. White and the other animal defenders who had joined forces on this issue. It passed a law stating that cattle must be shipped more humanely and given food and water. When the Pennsylvania Railroad refused to comply and continued to ship the animals in the old cruel ways, the Women's SPCA took on the whole railroad—they brought a suit against it on behalf of the cattle! The railroad finally agreed to obey the law.

Mrs. White's influence was international. She visited humane societies in Europe and once, while attending a Congress of Societies to Protect Animals held in Belgium, she aroused so much interest in her organization's City Pound and Dog Shelter that she was asked to write about it. Her article was distributed to humane organizations all over the world.

In 1876, Angell and Bergh and other leaders of the new humane societies and SPCAs nationwide formed the American Humane Association, a federation of animal welfare agencies, which is still in existence. The member organizations banded together to press for animal protection laws, spread humane education, and encourage shelter development and other concerns. You can be sure Caroline Earle White was a member and in fact served as vice president.

Today, after 110 years, the Women's SPCA of Pennsylvania, as it is now called, is still very much alive and continues to have an all-female board of directors. It has never turned away any animal brought to its doors.

Many of the early humane organizations focused on the plight of the thousands of workhorses in cities. One terrible problem these animals faced was that after a lifetime of hard work, when they became too tired and ill to pull wagons any longer, their owners replaced them with younger animals. Then the old horses were simply neglected, allowed to starve to death, or turned out to roam the streets helplessly on their own, without food or shelter.

One Philadelphia woman, Anne Waln Ryerss, left money in her will specifically to set up and maintain a hospital for "ill, aged, and injured animals." After her death in 1888, the Ryerss' Infirmary for Dumb Animals was founded, mostly for the permanent care of horses who could no longer work. The horses came from many sources and in all conditions. Some were found wandering the streets; some were taken from people who had mistreated them; and others were surrendered by owners who did not wish to keep them or kill them but wanted them to live out their final years in comfort. At Ryerss', it was not unusual for a fine horse who had pulled a fire wagon for many years to be stabled next to a pitiful cart horse whose owner had driven it nearly to death. (See Chapter 7.)

A Massachusetts woman, Harriet G. Bird, also proved to be a good friend to horses. In 1903, she donated her farm as a retirement haven for old workhorses. Hundreds of worn-out police and fire department horses passed their last years in peace and comfort there, as did many cart and carriage horses who had been abused or abandoned. A list of horses received at Red Acre Farm in one month in the fall of 1907, for example, reads as follows:

Oct. 1   Gray horse, one eye gone, thin and lame,
         25 years old
Oct. 4   Bay mare, thin, bruised, knees cut open,
         25 years
Oct. 25 Bay horse, thin, and lame, 20 years
         Bay horse, kidney trouble, 28 years
         Bay horse, thin, lame, and sick, 27 years
         Bay mare, spavined, emaciated, starved,
         27 years

Mrs. Bird was active in humane work until her death at age ninety-two. Today, Red Acre Farm still shelters a few horses, but its main activity is as a training center for hearing ear dogs for the deaf.

It is not unusual for a city to have several humane organizations that shelter animals, work to prevent cruelty, and conduct humane education and other projects that help animals. In 1899, Anna Harris Smith, a Boston woman with the same ideas as George Angell, felt that there was such a tremendous need for animal protection that the city could use another humane organization in addition to the Massachusetts SPCA. She named hers the Animal Rescue League of Boston, and like other groups, it devoted much of its early work to helping workhorses.

The Women's Pennsylvania SPCA had opened a clinic in Philadelphia where poor workingmen of that city could obtain free veterinary care for their horses. The Animal Rescue League of Boston opened a similar hospital in 1913 and also offered an important inducement to the owners of workhorses. It would lend healthy horses to needy people whose own horses were too sick to work and had to remain in the hospital temporarily. If a man had only one horse and depended on it for his livelihood, he simply couldn't afford for it to be out of service—his family might go hungry in the meantime. Therefore, a horse owner would certainly be tempted to keep working his animal, no matter how sick, old, or injured it might be. The fact that he could borrow a strong, healthy horse to use while his own animal recovered often made the difference between seeking treatment for his horse or letting it suffer.

Anna Harris Smith's concern for horses didn't diminish her work of helping the starving, lost, or abandoned dogs and cats of Boston. She was the first to deal with a form of cruelty that still persists in many places—the tendency of people to acquire pets at summer resorts and then desert them when the time comes to return to the city. People from the Animal Rescue League routinely combed the beach resorts near Boston at the end of every summer, gathering up the starving pets whose owners had abandoned them.

Mrs. Smith also took a worldwide view of animal suffering. Under her guidance, the Animal Rescue League of Boston opened branches in other Massachusetts cities and eventually went on to aid animal welfare organizations in other countries such as India, Japan, and Turkey. This energetic and dedicated woman ran the league personally until her death in 1929 at eighty-seven.

In 1899, another woman decided that the animals of her city, Chicago, could use another society to protect them. The Illinois Humane Society was already doing its best, but Rose Fay Thomas, wife of the conductor of the Chicago Symphony, felt that the plight of Chicago's animals was urgent. So she gathered a group together (again, all women) and founded an organization they named the Anti-Cruelty Society. Within five years it had opened a shelter for stray dogs and cats. It continues to serve Chicago's animals, and in fact opened a new shelter in 1982.

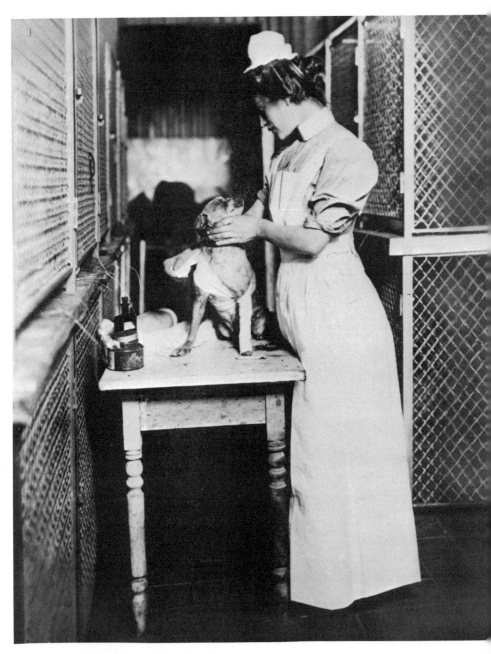

Veterinary medicine, animal shelters, and nurses' uniforms have changed, but compassion for injured animals is found in all civilized people. *Courtesy of Bide-A-Wee Home Association*

In the first decades of the twentieth century, the movement for establishing humane organizations and animal shelters continued all over the United States. Some of the agencies took the name SPCA or Humane Society along with the name of their city—for example, San Francisco SPCA, Atlanta Humane Society. Others have the name of their state: New Hampshire SPCA, Michigan Humane Society. Some have designations such as Erie County SPCA, Denver Dumb Friends League, or Animal Rescue League of Western Pennsylvania. Henry Bergh's group exists only in New York City and has kept the name American SPCA, or ASPCA. Today, New York City also has two other major, private shelters: the Bide-A-Wee Home Association and the Humane Society of New York.

A great tradition had been started by Henry Bergh, George Angell, Caroline Earle White, and the other compassionate and dedicated men and women who stemmed the tide of animal abuse. These people were the pioneers in a difficult and unpopular cause, and they deserve to be honored. They had to endure ridicule and indifference, but they managed to greatly diminish the indiscriminate and total abuse of animals, and they pointed the way to a more enlightened and civilized treatment of our fellow creatures. The work they began is ours to continue.

Henry Bergh died in his bed in the winter of 1888 while a fierce blizzard swirled outside his windows, and perhaps the animals in heaven welcomed him. A large funeral was held and many wreaths of flowers were banked around his coffin. One wreath of roses framed a picture of a big dog, and the inscription read: To Henry Bergh, Samson's best friend.

One day in 1909 when George Angell was eighty-six years old, he put the finishing touches on an editorial he had written for *Our Dumb Animals*. It was his last act on earth. Angell's funeral was distinguished by an impressive display

For centuries, the riderless horse has appeared in funerals as a gesture of respect for a fallen leader. Thirty-eight riderless horses were led in George Angell's funeral in 1909 to symbolize his love for them. *Courtesy of Massachusetts SPCA*

of the animals he had given a large part of his life for: thirty-eight horses in quiet procession, following his body to the cemetery.

When Caroline Earle White died in 1916 at age eighty-three, letters honoring her poured in from all over the world. She had been a tower of strength to others.

The revolutionary reforms of the 1860s and 1870s have never quite been equaled. The mood of indignation against cruelty to animals that swept the country then has not been repeated. Progress toward a humane world for all of us, people and other animals alike, seems to take place in bursts, followed by lulls when very little happens, or when gains may be lost. Perhaps there will be another surge of humaneness in our time.

The Fight
Against Dogfighting

JANE, THE HUMANE INVESTIGATOR, was having a conference with Lynne and Jeffrey, lawyers who worked part-time for the SPCA in our story.

"I gave the man a summons," reported Jane. "We took photos of the dog after it was put to sleep here. Dr. Buckley's report indicated it was starved, neglected, and suffering from exposure. I wish I'd been able to get a photo of the doghouse the animal was chained to—it was just a pile of sticks. That owner should not get away with treating a dog that way. Jail is too good—I'd like to see him sentenced to live in that doghouse for a while."

"We'll do our best," Jeffrey told her. "But even if we get to court and win, we'll probably not be able to get much more than a fine against him."

"He should be prohibited from owning dogs," said Jane. "Just being brought to court and fined probably won't make him treat animals any better."

Laws that apply to cases of animal abuse vary from place to place and usually do not impose severe punishments on people who are found guilty. So even though an attorney prosecuting an animal cruelty case often wins, he or she usually has to be satisfied with a small victory. Generally, animal abusers only have to pay fines or perhaps perform some service in their communities—they are very rarely sentenced to jail.

Also, much depends on an individual judge. Some judges feel that human concerns are the only ones worthy of the time and attention of our courts, so they won't even agree to hear cases of animal abuse. There are many laws on the books that are intended to protect animals, but getting these laws obeyed and enforced, and getting people who break the laws punished, are problems that all people involved in humane work must deal with continually.

However, both Lynne and Jeffrey, like many of today's attorneys who are interested in animal rights law, were skillful lawyers. Both of them had had experience in criminal law, which often proved helpful in prosecuting cruelty cases.

Only recently, Lynne had won a case that sent a man to jail for mutilating a cat with an ax.

"You're not going to believe this, but my next-door neighbor has just cut his cat's paws off!" a woman's voice had cried over the telephone at the shelter. "Please come! The animal is suffering horribly!"

Fortunately, Jane was not out on another call when this desperate report had come in. She didn't lose any time getting to the address. She rushed the dying cat back to the shelter, where Dr. Buckley put it out of its agony.

Then Jane interviewed the woman who had reported the incident.

"I was out working in my garden when I saw Roy, my

neighbor, come running out of his house cursing and yelling and carrying his cat. The cat was trying to get away, but Roy had a grip on it and was shouting 'I'll teach you to scratch!' or something like that. He rushed into his garage. I've never seen him so mad."

She paused for a minute, shuddering. "I'll never forget the sounds that cat made, coming from the garage. I couldn't imagine what was happening, but the screams were horrible. Then there was a silence. Roy came out and stamped into his house. I was afraid to go look in the garage, so I just went on working, though I was really upset. But in a little while the cat came stumbling out, trailing blood and dragging itself crazily. It crept under a bush at the edge of our property. And then"—the woman's eyes were wide with horror as she continued—"I looked under the bush and the cat was lying there. I could see its front legs were just bloody stumps. Roy must have used an ax to chop off its paws. That's when I phoned the SPCA."

"You did the right thing," Jane reassured her. "There's no telling how long the cat would have suffered before it died. It was still conscious when I found it."

"My husband will probably be angry with me for reporting Roy. He'll say I should have minded my own business," the woman sighed shakily. "But I don't care. I couldn't just ignore that cat."

Jane's next act was to get a search warrant and enter the garage. The man had not yet cleaned up after his bloody act, so Jane was able to seize enough damaging evidence to provide Lynne with what she needed to make a good case against Roy. The people in the courtroom were sickened, and this judge was sharp. He not only fined the man but sentenced him to jail for a year.

Lynne and Jeffrey handled a variety of cases for the

SPCA. Sometimes there were cruelty prosecutions, such as the cases against the owner of the frozen and starved dog and the man who had cut off his cat's paws. Sometimes the lawyers gave advice to owners who had legal questions involving their pets; other times they defended people whose landlords had suddenly ordered them to get rid of their pets or move out—even when the pets hadn't created any nuisance or bothered anyone.

A few SPCAs have full-time lawyers on their staffs; most have none and even have difficulty finding attorneys who will take cases for them. Slowly, however, animals are being accorded some standing in the view of our courts.

One legal battle Lynne and Jeffrey were now getting involved in was as secret and full of suspense as the most dangerous detective work. The SPCA was joining with humane investigators in another part of the state, along with a national humane organization, to try to crack a large dogfighting ring.

The "sport" of pitting animals against each other in gory battles for the amusement of crowds of spectators and gamblers has existed for several thousand years. The Romans, for example, held vast spectacles in which lions, elephants, bears, and other wild animals were driven into the arenas to fight each other or human slaves. Animals that survived these bloody battles were often then killed by archers from the grandstand who paid for the privilege of shooting at the injured animals still standing among the dead.

For hundreds of years in England, the practice of turning dogs loose on a chained bear was considered lots of fun and drew big crowds. Another "sport" was letting dogs attack a chained bull, and a special breed of dog was developed for it—the ancestor of the bulldog. (Today's comical-looking bulldogs, however, are usually gentle and are not the breed used in dogfighting.)

Most people think of animal fights as spectacles of by-gone times. Or, if they have heard of dogfighting at all, they think it is a rare backwoods exhibition participated in by a very few people. They are wrong.

This primitive activity thrives today as a sort of underworld gambling "sport." Fighting dogs, called pit dogs, pit bull terriers, American pit bull terriers, or just pit bulls, are bred and sold, trained and taught, and entered in fights, often with large sums of money bet on them. There are many

A pit bull terrier. *Courtesy of Humane Society of the United States*

published dogfighting journals and newsletters. Anywhere from one hundred to three hundred men, women, and children attend these contests, which are frequently held in the dead of night in secret places, usually surrounded by armed men who keep a lookout for the police.

Occasionally, humane agents together with various law enforcement officers may, through careful undercover detective work, discover where a fight is being held. Then they'll raid it, arresting the participants and sometimes the spectators, depending on the law in the particular state. But actually, most dogfighters have little to fear. Dogfighting is illegal in every state, and yet it is on the increase. The laws against it are very rarely enforced, and most people involved in it are never punished.

People who go in for dogfighting are often those who have little success or recognition in their lives, so they try to get it through their dogs. The violence of the fights provides a release for their frustrations.

Dogfighters pursue this "sport" with passionate interest and see nothing wrong in what they are doing. They claim they love their dogs. The breeding and selling of pit dogs is a nationwide occupation, and the dogs are often expensive. Even though most people who own these animals use them for fighting rather than showing, the dogs are recognized by the pure-breed kennel associations as Staffordshire bull terriers or American Staffordshire terriers. This recognition unfortunately has the appearance of sanctioning dogfighting and making it respectable.

Pit dogs are trained like athletes. Their owners make them work out every day, often running them for hours on treadmills so that they become strong and fit. Early in their training they may be allowed to kill cats or rabbits to give them a taste for blood. The small animal is hung alive just over the dogs' heads; and dogs jump and tear at it till it is dead.

Sometimes the young dogs are allowed to practice on ordinary nonfighting dogs that are kept just for this sorry purpose, or they are allowed to fight each other in short practice fights called "rolls." Pit dogs may be friendly enough with people, but they are programmed by heredity and training to attack each other, and other animals, and fight to kill.

When an owner decides a dog is ready for the real thing, he or she enters it in a scheduled fight. These fights are for money—and may involve half a million dollars in fees and bets. Humane officers would like to see dogfighting brought to an end because of the cruelty involved. Law enforcement officers are interested mainly because of the illegal weapons, drug traffic, and other criminal activity that goes on at dogfights.

At a fight, two dogs are taken to a "pit"—an enclosure about 14 feet square with a wall 2 or 3 feet high around it. Before the match, each dog is washed to be sure poison that would affect its opponent during a bite hasn't been rubbed into its coat. (Sometimes, however, the dogs have been injected by their owners with drugs to make them fight harder.)

Then the dogs are held facing each other in the pit, and when the signal is given, they rush at each other and are quickly locked in combat. These dogs don't bark, growl, snap, or snarl as ordinary dogs do when they get into a fight. Pit bulls sink their teeth into each other with their powerful jaws and hang on silently. The crowds make a lot of noise, but the only sounds coming from the dogs may be of bones being crushed. One dog may go for the face and throat of its opponent, while the other tries to break a limb or gouge out the stomach.

A fighting dog, his teeth sunk into his opponent's throat, hangs on with intent to kill. *Courtesy of Humane Society of the United States*

In the pocket of the dogfighter in the foreground are pointed "pry sticks," used to separate dogs during deadly combat in the pit. *Photograph confiscated by the Michigan Humane Society in the course of that Society's investigation and prosecution of a conspiracy to dogfight case*

The owners separate their dogs with a sharp stick from time to time during a fight, so that the animals can rest and have the blood wiped from them. Sometimes a dog may be so hurt or exhausted that it refuses to continue the fight. But most often it will give all it's got, even with its bones broken and blood running into its eyes. A fight may last up to two hours.

Naturally, the owners of winning dogs are very proud of them and pleased with the money they collect. Dogs that lose may be taken out of the pit and shot or simply abandoned by their owners. About half of the dogs, even the winners, die of wounds and injuries after several fights. They are rarely taken to veterinarians for treatment, unless fighters know a vet who will close his or her eyes to the obvious. An experienced pit bull carries many permanent scars.

Humane investigators who attempt to tackle dogfighting usually operate on tips from informers, go undercover, assume false identities, and pretend to be interested in getting into dogfighting themselves. If they uncover enough evidence to interest law enforcement authorities, they may be joined by police officers or agents from the prosecuting attorney's office, or—if drugs are involved—the FBI. (The Department of Agriculture, which technically is supposed to be enforcing our federal laws against dogfighting, has never prosecuted a dogfighter.)

An investigator may take as long as a year collecting evidence before he or she brings in the authorities to raid a fight. And all the while the investigation is under cover, the humane agent is in danger of being hurt or even killed if his or her real identity is discovered. It is no job for amateurs.

When a dogfight ring is uncovered and a raid is made, the pit bull terriers are taken by the humane society. Some dogs are so badly hurt that it is necessary to euthanize them. The surviving dogs are usually dangerous to other dogs, cats, and other animals. Even dogs that are normally good-natured around people have been known to turn on them. Generally, pit bulls can't be trusted, and therefore don't make good pets, so humane shelters are reluctant to take chances with them, and often euthanize even those that survive the fights.

Some shelters that acquire pit bull terriers, either through a raid or from owners who surrender them, will retain ownership of the animals permanently and adopt them out only in a foster-care arrangement. A person who wants a pit bull from such a shelter can only become its guardian, after filling out extensive application forms and agreeing to allow the humane society to visit and examine the dog at any time. The humane society can take the dog back if there are any suspicious signs that the dog may be mistreated or used for fighting.

The fate of dogs has been in the hands of human beings for many thousands of years. Dogs are loyal friends and helpers, companions and protectors, and given half a chance they deeply love their owners. Dogs may quite normally fight and scrap with one another sometimes, but rarely do they fight to harm or kill—they fight to establish dominance. It is sad enough that dogs are turned into weapons against people, as guard dogs are. Somehow it is even more grotesque when by careful breeding and diligent training they become killers of their own kind.

Cockfighting, another form of entertainment that was once commonplace and is now underground, is also a target of today's humane societies and SPCAs. It features cocks specially bred to be fighters. The owners of these beautiful but ferocious birds fasten sharp spurs on their feet so that they can literally rip one another apart in a fight, and of course bets are placed on these bloody matches as well.

When Henry Bergh bounded into the street to stop the arm of the horse beater, when Caroline Earle White took the

Pennsylvania Railroad to court for shipping cattle under cruel conditions, when men and women everywhere began to interfere with those who were causing animals to suffer, they began a movement that went beyond sheltering. Many humane societies today try to defend animals against all kinds of cruelty, but in order for them to be effective, our law enforcement agencies and courts must know that the people of a community want the mistreatment of animals stopped.

7

Who Lives, Who Dies?

As Bill came to work, the phone at the front desk was ringing. It was only eight in the morning, early for people to start calling the animal shelter. A man was on the phone, sounding very upset.

"Have you got a black Labrador there named Kate?" he asked.

Bill remembered the sad dog that had been surrendered by a woman earlier in the week. But the previous two days had been his days off, so he didn't know what had happened to the dog in the meantime. Had she been adopted? That was always possible, in spite of her age. Had she been euthanized? That was unlikely; unless a dog was sick or injured, Karen Hamilton would keep it longer than two days, to give it a chance.

"We did have a dog like that brought in a few days ago," Bill said. "Hold on a minute and I'll check to see if she's still here."

He looked in the card file that kept a current record of all

60

the animals in the shelter at any given time. According to that, Kate was still here, but sometimes the persons who kept the card file were careless. Just to double-check, Bill hurried back to the dog kennels. Sure enough, lying disconsolately in her cage was Kate.

"Yes, we have a ten-year-old female black Labrador named Kate," Bill reported. "The woman who owned her brought her in three days ago."

"That was my mother, but the dog belonged to all of us. I didn't realize she was going to take Kate to a shelter!" exclaimed the man at the other end of the telephone. "Listen, can you hold on to my dog? I just found out about this. I'm going to drive over and get her, but it will take me about four hours. I'm calling from out of town. Don't do anything to Kate in the meantime, okay?"

"I'll put a *hold* card on her cage right away," promised Bill. He hung up the phone feeling good. But he was puzzled. If this fellow wanted Kate, why had his mother given her up in the first place? Bill mentioned the conversation to Mrs. Hamilton as soon as she arrived.

"Maybe this man hadn't realized his parents didn't want to keep the family dog," suggested Mrs. Hamilton. "Or maybe the woman didn't understand that her son would take Kate. There must be a serious lack of communication in that · family!

"But I'm so glad he's coming," she continued. "The dog is heartbroken. She isn't eating. People coming to adopt dogs have walked right by her because she is so unresponsive and disinterested."

Shortly after noon, a young man came hurrying into the shelter. Mrs. Hamilton led him back to Kate's cage.

"Kate!" he called as the shelter manager opened the cage. "Come here, girl! It's me!"

The black dog lifted her head, looked, and couldn't seem

to believe her eyes for a few seconds. Then she flung herself on the man, shaking all over and sobbing, wagging her tail until it looked as though it would come unattached from her body.

"She'll have to get used to living in an apartment and to being home alone during the day while I'm at work," said the man, hugging his ecstatic dog. "But I would never have given her away. I had no idea my parents were serious about not wanting her anymore."

"It's a good thing you came," said Mrs. Hamilton. "She's too old to have a very good chance of being adopted. And she has been depressed, almost determined to let herself die."

"Well, she's going to live with me now," said Kate's owner. As he left with Kate loping happily beside him on a leash, everyone in the shelter was smiling.

Isadora could not get used to living in a cage and paced about restlessly much of the time. But she hadn't given up hope. Whenever she heard someone approaching the aisle where her cage was, she would peer out, reaching her paw through the bars and crying plaintively.

The shelter workers treated her kindly enough, fed her, and cleaned her cage, but they had little time to pet her or talk to her. Jody, the volunteer, sometimes took her out and held her for a while, but Jody was in college and her hours at the shelter were limited.

People came every day to adopt pets, but most of them didn't stop long at Isadora's cage in spite of her pleas. One woman had paused.

"This seems like a nice cat," she remarked to the man with her.

"But she's eight years old," her companion pointed out, reading the card attached to the cage. "And she's not particularly beautiful. There's a tabby over there that's prettier and only a year old." And so they passed up Isadora.

Several evenings a week before Mrs. Hamilton went home, it was her job to select the animals that were to be euthanized early the next morning by Dr. Buckley's assistant, a veterinary technician, aided by one of the animal handlers. This was necessary to make room for the steady stream of new dogs and cats that were always coming in.

A shelter staff member gives the last meal to dogs and cats on death row. Their only crime is that nobody adopted them.

The shelter staff member hugs a dog headed for euthanasia.

In general, animals are chosen for euthanasia on the basis of health, youth, disposition, and appeal—the same criteria that determine their chances for adoption. Sick and seriously injured animals, such as the abused dog and cat, are euthanized right away to prevent their suffering further. But in some overburdened big-city shelters, minor health problems can also send an animal to its death. Ear mites, for example (a feline disorder that's easy to treat and cure), may be reason enough to relegate cats to euthanasia. Pets with handicaps such as deafness or a limp also usually lose their lives, for their adoption chances are poor.

As Karen Hamilton pointed out in referring to Kate and Isadora, even healthy pets of middle age may have to go. On the other hand, very young kittens are often euthanized, too, because, unless a shelter has staff members or volunteers who will take care of them at home, they sometimes don't do well in shelters without their mothers.

Dogs and cats that are shy and fearful are likely to be unadoptable because most people choosing pets, of course, want friendly ones. Shelter workers often try to socialize such animals by petting them, playing with them, and giving them a chance to warm up. But if the animals don't learn to trust people fairly soon, it is more humane to euthanize them than to keep them indefinitely in cages. Prolonged cage life has a bad effect on all animals. Dogs and cats have lived with people for so many thousands of years that the human home is now their natural habitat. Being caged up for a long time causes tremendous stress and emotional damage. Some become depressed and withdrawn and give up trying to live; others become restless and crazed.

Dogs and cats that bite or scratch are unadoptable for obvious reasons. The sad part is that a biting or scratching animal may be a normally gentle pet that is simply hysterical with fear and anxiety over being kept in the confusing atmosphere of a shelter. Was Tiger once a loving pet? There was no way of knowing. But unless a pet can be trusted to be friendly in a new home, a humane society can't take a chance on letting it be adopted.

What all this means is that today, nationwide, *most* of the animals, 70 to 80 percent, in a humane society or SPCA shelter never leave. Some 13 million pets go through shelters each year, of which about 10 million must be killed. That means over a thousand pets die every hour that passes.

Some shelters do not euthanize. They manage by accepting only animals that they have room for, and by accepting only those that are adoptable. If a shelter is privately run and receives no public funds, it can afford to be choosy. When such a shelter happens to find itself with an unadoptable pet, it sends the animal to the pound or another shelter. It can truthfully advertise that it doesn't put animals to sleep, and the public, who doesn't understand the problem, thinks this is great and prefers to give donations of money to that shelter. But when a shelter makes this claim, other shelters by contrast look bad, as if the people in them euthanize pets because they are cruel or because they don't try to find homes for them.

SPCAs and humane societies that accept any and all animals, that have no waiting lists, and that never turn away an animal are forced to euthanize. They receive many unadoptable pets. And in spite of all their efforts to increase adoptions, they still have many more pets than people can or will adopt.

At least one humane agency, the National Cat Protection Society in Long Beach, California, has a retirement center where, for a fee, a cat owner can place a healthy pet with the assurance that it will never be euthanized. If the cat is not

A twenty-nine-year-old horse that for many years led military funerals at Arlington National Cemetery now grazes in peaceful retirement at Ryerss'.

adopted, it will live out its life not in a cage but in a large, pleasant enclosure among other cats.

Ryerss' Infirmary for Dumb Animals still exists as an alternative to death for a fortunate number of aged or abused horses. In 1956, the present site was purchased—a 200-

For the rest of their lives, an elderly horse and a shaggy pony will get all the love they need, especially from the child of the assistant superintendent, at Ryerss'.

acre farm in the Pennsylvania countryside. A horse, given good care, can live to age thirty, maybe a little longer. Here, a twenty-five-year-old former police horse grazes contentedly next to a thirty-year-old pinto that came from an SPCA. Two elderly show ponies share a pasture with a little donkey that had been taken from an owner who had abused her. At any given time, some forty or fifty old horses, ponies, and donkeys are cared for at Ryerss'.

Why are there such huge numbers of pets in shelters? One reason is that so many people let their pets breed, like the woman who brought in Luke Skywalker and his brothers and sister and refused to have the mother cat spayed.

The main reason, though, is that most people, like Snoopy's family, regard a pet as a disposable object, something to discard whenever it becomes inconvenient to keep it. Some studies have indicated that 40 percent of all dogs and 30 percent of all cats are given away by their owners. Too few people think of a pet as a living, thinking, feeling creature that they are responsible for for the duration if its life.

Paradoxically, the shelters perpetuate the problem. They have to serve as a dumping ground for people's unwanted pets because otherwise the animals would be abandoned, but ironically, this encourages people to keep on dumping pets in shelters.

Studies of pets and pet ownership reveal that the vast majority of dogs and cats are killed, by people, long before they reach old age. Human beings can cause the death of their animals either through cruelty and neglect, as in the case of the abused dog and cat, or by allowing them to roam free. Unsupervised pets usually get killed by cars or in other accidents; some die at the hands of sadistic people. And pets whose owners surrender them to animal shelters may be euthanized.

Deciding who will live and who will die is a painful problem for shelter employees. While some get to the point where they can keep their feelings under control and make the choices coolly and unemotionally, others are haunted. Many shelter employees, even those who do not have to make the decisions or actually watch the dying, can't take it after a while. Just being around so many pets that they know will have to be destroyed upsets them, and they resign from their jobs. In fact, people who love animals often apply for work at shelters, are hired, and then quit after just one day.

One thing that helps shelter workers do their jobs, however, is the fact that euthanasia methods are much more humane today than they were in the past. After the members of the Women's Pennsylvania SPCA put a stop to clubbing animals to death in the pounds of Philadelphia, various euthanasia methods were developed and tried in shelters everywhere, including gas and electrocution. One method still in use today in some places is the decompression chamber. Animals are loaded into a sealed container from which the air is quickly pumped out. The animals become unconscious and die from lack of oxygen. It is possible, however, that they may suffer acute panic, discomfort, and even pain before they pass out. For this reason, the better humane societies no longer use the decompression chamber. And humane activists have succeeded in getting the decompression chamber outlawed in several states.

The method that offers the least chance of pain and fear to an animal is by injection of sodium pentobarbital. This requires two people—one to hold the animal and the other to give the injection. But if the animal is gently soothed so that it doesn't become afraid, it has no idea what is happening. The injection itself is virtually painless, and the animal experiences only drowsiness. It is literally "put to sleep."

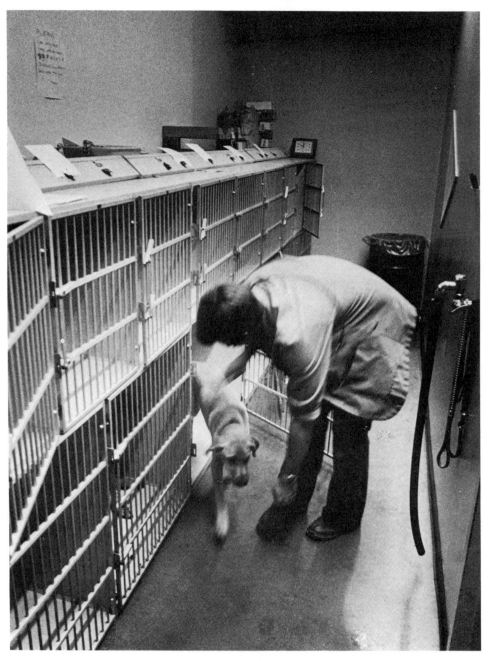

Abandoned by his owner, too long rejected by potential adopters, a dog heads for euthanasia.

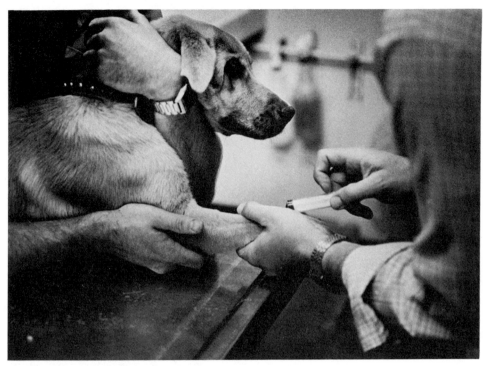

Given an injection of sodium pentobarbital, he grows drowsy, dies, and is added to the day's lineup.

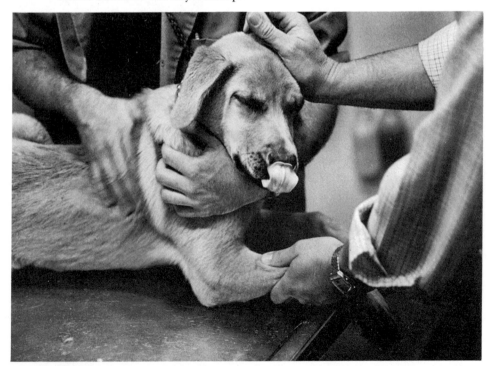

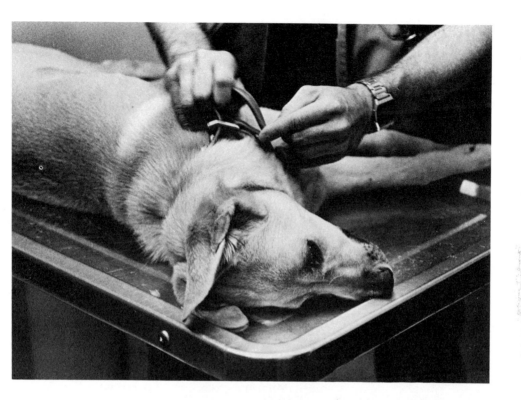

Karen Hamilton hated the part of her job that required her to select which pets had to go. But she knew the decision had to be made. Otherwise, the shelter would quickly be overflowing with animals that it had no room for and couldn't afford to feed and care for.

She knew that time was running out for Isadora, Tim, and Tiger, whose chances for adoption were not the best. Tim's injury was nearly healed, he was eating well and beginning to put on weight since he had been rid of his worms, but nobody had given a thought to adopting him because he was still so shy. The shelter workers reported that though Tim never growled or showed his teeth at anyone, he still drew back and cowered whenever someone attempted to touch him. He never wagged his tail or came when called.

Mrs. Hamilton walked to his cage and looked at him with sympathy. Given time in a home where he was loved and well treated, Tim would probably turn into a wonderful pet. Would someone come along and give him that home?

Tim, who had been sleeping, lifted his head and met Mrs. Hamilton's eyes as if he knew her thoughts. The shelter manager knelt down and put her hand into the cage. "Here, boy," she coaxed. "Come. Nobody's going to hurt you."

The dog hesitated. Then, still on his belly, he crawled to the woman's outstretched hand, sniffed it, and then gave it a little lick.

Mrs. Hamilton stood up and went on by. She did not write *Euth* on Tim's card. He would live at least one more day.

Animal Control

WHEN THE WOMEN'S Pennsylvania SPCA per-
suaded the mayor of Philadelphia to let them take over the
pound, turn it into a shelter, and assume the job of employ-
ing the dogcatchers who rounded up the city's strays, they
set an important precedent. Today, over a hundred years
later, in most cities the SPCA or another humane shelter organization functions as the city pound and has the contract
for animal control. The symbolic SPCA in this book is also
the pound.

However, in numerous places, the pound is a quite separate place.

Pounds, remember, existed in the cities of the United
States long before the early humanitarians founded the
SPCAs, humane societies, animal rescue leagues, anticruelty
societies, and other animal protection and shelter agencies.
They were places where wandering or homeless dogs were
brought in order to rid the streets of them. The purpose of
pounds was to protect the health and comfort of the cities'

75

people, not to shelter homeless pets and put them up for adoption.

There was great fear of rabies (once called hydrophobia) in those days. Occasionally a stray dog did indeed develop rabies and become a danger to people. However, any dog that acted upset was suspect, and vast numbers of dogs were captured and brutally killed who did not have the dread disease at all.

Today, pounds are still supported by the government of their cities or counties. Most of them have improved since the nineteenth century, but conditions in them vary widely from city to city. Some are clean and well kept and afford decent treatment to the impounded animals. Others are atrocious concentration camps for animals. Most pounds fall somewhere in between.

The dogcatchers of old have been replaced by today's animal control officers. They are far better trained and generally more humane than their nineteenth-century predecessors, who were usually ignorant, incompetent, often brutal men. Now, many men and women in animal control work are skilled professionals who do a good job rounding up stray animals and rescuing those in trouble.

Pounds are required to keep strays for several days to give owners a chance to reclaim them, if indeed they ever had owners. Unfortunately, sometimes animals are euthanized immediately by careless workers before their owners have had a chance to claim them. Occasionally, owners of lost dogs and cats do come looking for their pets and bail them out, and sometimes people adopt pets from pounds.

If an SPCA or other humane society doubles as the pound, it receives some money from the city or county for performing the animal control work. If a city has several large humane shelter agencies, they might take turns receiving the contract for animal control. And in other cities, the

A lost dog is captured by an animal control officer. Fortunately, he is wearing up-to-date license tags, so the officer can trace the owner.

The officer delivers the lucky dog to his lucky owner, who is relieved to have her pet home safe and sound. Both have narrowly escaped tragedy—the dog could easily have been killed by a car or in some other accident.

animal control officers may work for the police or some other city department but bring the animals they collect to the local SPCA or humane society shelter.

Here and there, in a small community, a local humanitarian may open up a shelter and get the contract to act as the pound, but not be able to provide good conditions for the animals. A shelter needs far more than the animal control money it gets from a local government. Unless it has a capable administrator and generous financial support, it may be a dirty, shabby place, with animals kept under horrible conditions.

Throughout the United States there are hundreds of private shelters, large and small, that are not the city, county, or state SPCAs. These are usually small havens set up and run by kind people who work with devotion and dedication, taking in unwanted pets and trying to find homes for them. Some of these shelters are very good and may even have private clinics for low-cost animal care and spay/neutering.

The people in charge have a lot to do with the quality of a shelter. If the director is sensitive to animals, an efficient business manager, and skilled at initiating creative projects that will attract the attention and support of the community, the animals benefit. However, even the most sincere, capable, and hardworking shelter director can't create a good facility without the help of the community. It is up to the citizens of every community to see that the shelters and pounds are decent places.

Some shelters in economically depressed parts of the country have to struggle to give even minimal care to lost, abandoned, or unwanted animals. They are often run by caring but overworked people. They may have the contract to do animal control for several neighboring towns but have no ambulance and no veterinarian. Because they are usually overcrowded and have so little funds, most strays must be

An animal control officer, who has rescued a kitten that was trapped in a drainpipe, praises the young girl who found him and called her to the scene.

Karen Hamilton's SPCA had several excellent volunteers, like Jody, and very caring employees. The director chose her staff carefully, looking for the combination of kindness mixed with responsibility that made a good shelter worker.

"Some people are here with a mother cat and three nursing kittens, and they want to give us the whole bunch," said Bill at the door of Mrs. Hamilton's office. "Also, a few minutes ago a man came in with a box, placed it on the counter, and before I could say anything, he rushed out. There's a young Siamese cat yowling away in the box."

"All right, put them all in the clinic where Dr. Buckley can examine them tomorrow," said Mrs. Hamilton. More cats. Several had come in earlier, and space was needed. She looked around the cat room with its rows of cages all filled with cats. She had already written *Euth* on the cards of a few who had been passed up for adoption for too long and were growing depresssed in their cages. She opened Tiger's cage.

"How are you doing, fellow?" She spoke soothingly to the big yellow cat who crouched at the back. Tiger had cleaned himself up and was beginning to look handsome. But he still hadn't recovered from his fright or his mistrust of human beings. As Mrs. Hamilton put her hand toward him, he snarled, sprang at her, and raked her hand with his claws.

The shelter manager sighed. It would take too long to socialize this cat and help him get over his fear. There was no way of knowing how long it would be before Tiger could safely be offered for adoption—if ever. Even if someone wanted to take a chance on him, the likelihood was too great that he would be returned, or abandoned, because of his unstable disposition.

Reluctantly, Mrs. Hamilton wrote *Euth* on his card. She felt she had no choice.

Just then, an elderly woman came into the cat room and began walking down the aisles, looking at all the cats and reading the cards attached to their cages.

"Can I help you?" asked Mrs. Hamilton.

"I would like to adopt a cat," said the woman. "My old fellow just died two weeks ago and I miss him terribly."

Her eyes misted with tears.

Mrs. Hamilton wasn't sure what the woman meant by "my old fellow." Could it be her husband, or a man friend? She waited for the lady to continue.

"His name was Willow because he was so slim and lively when he was a kitten," said the elderly woman. "He lived to see his twentieth birthday last month," she added with a touch of pride.

Mrs. Hamilton smiled. "Well, we have lots of nice cats here who need homes. Do you want any particular color?"

"Any color is all right, but I don't want a young cat—I don't want a pet that will outlive me," announced the woman firmly. "I'd like a middle-aged cat."

"We have just the cat for you," said Mrs. Hamilton. "She's very sweet, but everybody has passed her up because she's eight years old." She led the woman to Isadora's cage.

Isadora pressed herself against the bars and reached out her paw. "Mew!" she pleaded, looking directly at the older woman. "Mew!"

Mrs. Hamilton opened the cage and lifted the cat into the woman's arms. Isadora began to purr loudly and rub her head against the woman's hand. She looked into her face and mewed.

"I'll take her," said the elderly lady.

It had been a busy day at the SPCA shelter. Fourteen dogs and cats had been brought in, including the newborn kittens. Several dogs and cats had been adopted. A few, like poor hostile Tiger, had lived their last day on earth.

Princess Leia, one of the four kittens that had come in the same day as Snoopy, had been adopted by a ten-year-old girl and her mother. They had paid a deposit—promising to bring her back for her spay operation when she was old enough—and had gone home armed with pamphlets on proper cat care.

Snoopy had settled in and acted as if he would be happy enough to live at the shelter forever—he was treated better here than in the home he had come from. He had been moved into a larger cage with two other pups and was glad to have the companionship.

For Kate and Isadora, it had been a wonderful day.

"Imagine!" said Mrs. Hamilton to Bill as they closed up the front desk for the night. "Two miracles in one day. A ten-year-old dog has been reclaimed, and an eight-year-old cat has been adopted. I wish we had surprises like this more often.

"By the way, Bill," she continued. "The woman who took Isadora gave me an idea. Let's institute a plan to encourage the adoption of older pets by elderly people. The San Francisco SPCA has such a project. We might, for instance, charge anybody over sixty-five considerably less than our regular adoption fees—say, three dollars—if they take a dog or cat over two years old. Let's start such a program and see if we can get the newspapers, radio, and TV stations to publicize it. It might interest elderly people who would hesitate to take on a lively young dog or cat, or an untrained puppy, but would appreciate an older, more sedate animal."

"Sounds like a good idea," said Bill. "I wish we could also set up a support network to help older people who live alone take care of their pets if they need it. An emergency volunteer group who would be available to walk dogs when the sidewalks are icy, for example, or pick up pet food and litter in bad weather. I bet a lot of elderly people would enjoy the companionship of pets if they knew they could count on a little help with the animals' care if they needed it."

Karen Hamilton and Bill would find the ways to put these plans into effect. New ideas and creative programs are what help keep SPCAs and other shelter organizations alive and effective in their communities.

Pet Therapy Visits

ONE AFTERNOON at about five-thirty, Snoopy and the other puppies heard people coming into the kennel room, so they peered out of their cages to see what was going on. While the shelter was open late for adoptions a few days a week, the bustling activity was usually quieting down by this hour.

The pups were alert, however, having finished their after-dinner naps, and were delighted when three people opened the door to their cages. Snoopy was scooped up by one of them. Then he and his friends found themselves in small, square cages with handles on top.

They were whisked through the door, down the hall, out to the driveway, and placed in a station wagon. Next to their cages was one with Luke Skywalker, Han Solo, and a couple of other kittens in it. All the young animals gazed about them in wonder.

The three people—a woman, a girl of sixteen, and a young man of about twenty—got in, and the station wagon moved off into the night. The puppies and kittens stared at the lights going past outside. One of the puppies began to whimper a little.

"Don't be scared, little guy," said the man, opening the cage to pat him. "You'll have fun where we're going."

One of the projects the SPCA conducted in the community was a program of taking puppies and kittens on regular visits to nursing homes, hospitals, and other institutions where disabled people lived. These visits were called "pet therapy" because the young animals had such a beneficial effect on the patients. They not only cheered them up and entertained them—they often actually made them better.

Tonight Snoopy, Luke, and Han Solo, and the other pups and kittens were going to a nursing home where a great many old people were patients. Nina, the staff member at the shelter who was in charge of the pet therapy program, drove the station wagon; the high school girl and the man, a college student, were both volunteers who gave an evening a week to the pet therapy visits. As they pulled up at the nursing home, they were joined by two other volunteers who had come directly from their jobs to meet them there.

The recreation room of the nursing home was large but had little in it—just some chairs and couches, a big TV set, and a few small tables for patients who were able to sit and play cards. This evening, the room was filled Elderly men and women were seated everywhere, many of them in wheelchairs, waiting for the pets. Most of the people were very old and frail; some could not even wheel their own chairs but had been brought to the recreation room by nurses and aides.

Some of the patients began to smile as Nina and the volunteers placed the carrying cages on the floor in the center of the room. They took the puppies and kittens out and began to carry them around, stopping and holding them for every person to see and fondle. Those who wished to could hold the animals for a little while.

"The only time I ever get a chance to hug anybody is when you come," said one lady to a puppy, snuggling him in her arms.

An old man held out his hands for Snoopy. "Come here, boy," he said. "I once had a little dog just like you."

Wiggling with joy and wagging his tail, Snoopy scrambled up the man's chest and began to lick his chin. The man laughed and tickled Snoopy behind his ears.

A lady in a wheelchair next to the man lifted her head to look. She had been staring at the floor dejectedly ever since she had been brought into the recreation room, but her faded blue eyes began to light up as she watched Snoopy play in the arms of the man.

Nina came up to her with Han Solo in her arms. Han was a quiet kitten and as pretty as Princess Leia, his sister.

"Would you like to hold a kitten?" Nina asked the lady.

"I don't think she'll answer you," a nurse who was standing nearby said quietly to Nina. "She doesn't speak. She has been here three weeks and is so withdrawn we haven't been able to get any response from her, no matter how hard we try to draw her out."

Nina placed Han Solo gently in the woman's lap. The elderly lady looked at him for a minute and then began to stroke him. She was smiling faintly as she ran her thin hand over his fur, but tears began to roll down her cheeks.

Concerned, Nina started to remove Han Solo from the lady's lap. "Does the kitten make you feel sad?" she asked. But the woman held him close. "Or shall I leave him with you for a little while?" Nina quickly added.

"Yes," replied the aged woman softly. "I like cats." It was as if a lot of pent-up emotion was being released by the

An elderly woman in a nursing home is so moved by the sight and
feel of a little rabbit that she bursts into tears.

contact with the tiny animal, who curled up and began to
purr loudly.

The nurse looked at Nina and raised her eyebrows in surprise. "I think this is really helping her," she whispered.
"It's the first time she has noticed anything or spoken to anyone. It's good for her to express her feelings."

After a while, all the patients who wished to hold the pets
had had a turn, and the animals were beginning to get somewhat restless. Someone put Snoopy on the floor, and he immediately found one of the other puppies and challenged him
to a game. The two little dogs began to roll about and play-
wrestle, and the people watching them started to laugh.

"Let's put all the pets down and see what happens," suggested Nina to the volunteers. "Will someone please close the door to the room so none of them can run out?"

Luke Skywalker was not as handsome a kitten as his brother, but he made up for it in personality. He was fearless, curious, and lively. While Han Solo was a passive kitten who liked to sit and purr, Luke was extremely frisky. Now Luke ran after Snoopy and tried to catch his tail. Another puppy waggled up to join the fun. Luke let go of Snoopy's tail and took off after the other pup. Soon the kittens and puppies, all except Han, who was still half-asleep in the lap of the lady in the wheelchair, were engaged in rough-and-tumble play, and the audience was shaking with laughter. The more rowdy the young animals became, the louder the elderly people laughed.

Suddenly the door to the recreation room opened, and two men put their heads in. They looked at the circus going on in the middle of the room and listened to the bursts of laughter from the people watching.

"I've seen the visiting pets before, but I haven't heard laughter like this in the four years I've been administrator here," said one of the men.

The other man was one of the doctors who took care of the patients' medical needs. "I have to admit," he commented, "that this probably does these people as much good as anything I could prescribe—maybe more."

The lady who liked Han Solo so much looked sad when she had to give him up at the end of the evening.

"When can you come again?" the nurse asked Nina.

"We have visits scheduled to other places—it will be several weeks before we're back here," answered Nina. "But maybe I can arrange for a kitten to be brought here tomorrow or the day after, just to see this lady. I think she needs it." Though she didn't have many volunteers, and she herself

Aged hands enjoy holding a pet rabbit.

often worked late hours at the shelter, Nina would do her best to bring some healing joy in the form of a kitten to this woman. As Nina and the volunteers were leaving with the pets, the nurse spoke to her patient, and the lady answered her briefly. A breakthrough had been made. The lady was much more alert and responsive.

A few evenings later, Snoopy and his friends paid a visit to the children's ward of a hospital. Many of the youngsters were walking around in their bathrobes and eagerly reached for the pets to carry in their arms. Those children who were bedridden held the young animals and played with them in their beds, giggling, while the nurses and aides smiled with approval.

"When we first proposed these visits to the hospital superintendent, he said no," explained Nina to a new volunteer. "He insisted the pets would carry germs. He said they'd make messes for the nurses to clean up. But we showed him stories in magazines and newspapers about other hospitals where pets visit. We explained that only healthy and friendly animals are used, and the visits are timed sufficiently long after they have eaten so that accidents are extremely rare. We also showed this man several scholarly research papers that documented the benefits that people derive from pet therapy.

"Finally he decided to give us a try. Some of the nurses disapproved, but after a few visits, even they had to admit that the children's morale is tremendously improved by the pets. Even the kids who are very sick respond and seem to be helped."

A little girl in a hospital likes being tickled by something warm and fuzzy and alive.

All over the United States, it has become the practice of many animal shelter agencies to conduct pet therapy programs for nursing homes, hospitals, and other institutions for the elderly, sick, and handicapped in their communities. These programs are nearly always conducted by volunteers and arranged and supervised by a staff member of the shelter and the activities director of the nursing home or hospital. Most such places have directors in charge of recreation for the patients, and they often find it hard to provide fresh entertainment that the patients can enjoy. These directors are the ones most likely to be receptive to the idea of visiting pets. Life for most handicapped people who are confined to institutions is pretty dull and cheerless. However, pet therapy not only provides amusement and diversion, but, as in the case of the lady with Han Solo, actually seems to be therapeutic.

It is not at all uncommon for totally withdrawn people to speak for the first time when a puppy or kitten is placed in their arms. The pets have the effect of good medicine. The reasons for this are not yet fully understood, but scientists who are investigating the relationships of pets and human beings think that it is partly because the animals are so responsive and affectionate. They are not put off by old age or handicaps. They give instant love and approval, they make no demands, and they enjoy being stroked and cuddled. Most people, especially the old, ill, or disabled, need something to touch and fondle, even if only for a little while.

In some places, pets from shelters can be placed to live permanently as mascots in nursing homes and other residential facilities. Live-in pets obviously give much more pleasure to the patients than those that visit once every few weeks or months and then are taken away again.

Each mascot must be very carefully selected, and people who work in the residence where it is placed must be responsible to see that the animal is properly taken care of. The pet is shared by the patients, or residents, but the rights of those people who don't like animals must be respected. What generally happens is that persons who don't like pets simply ignore them, and the animals tend to spend their time with the people who like them.

Sometimes the pet is restricted to certain rooms; in other nursing homes it is allowed everywhere, except in the kitchens or dining areas, as required by the state health laws.

While most state laws that regulate nursing homes and other such residences do not prohibit live-in pets, some do. The hope is that these laws will be changed, so that any residence for elderly or handicapped people can have a pet or several pets, if the patients and the staff wish to.

Humane Education

ONE DAY, THE THIRD WEEK that Snoopy was in the SPCA, Nina put him in a carrying cage again. This time he was not going on another visit to a hospital or nursing home. Part of Nina's job was to teach humane education, and today she was going to be in a special school assembly program, speaking to first, second, and third graders about kindness to animals. Han Solo was also chosen to go, along with a white rabbit, a very calm adult cat, and a friendly adult dog who had had obedience training and could be counted on to put on a good performance for the schoolchildren.

When Snoopy was carried up on the stage, he was amazed to see so many kids. He wasn't at all afraid. His experiences at the hospital and nursing home had made him ready to trust anyone.

Part of Nina's program included a demonstration of the proper way to hold a puppy.

"Even though a mother dog might carry a newborn puppy by the scruff of the neck in her mouth, people should

96

never pick up a puppy that way, or they'll hurt it," she explained. She showed the children how to lift Snoopy and support him gently while holding him securely so he couldn't wiggle loose and fall.

"Kittens also should be picked up and held supporting their hind quarters," Nina went on. "Never by the scruff of the neck." And she let several children come up on the stage and take turns holding Snoopy and Han Solo properly.

A boy learns how to hold a kitten gently.

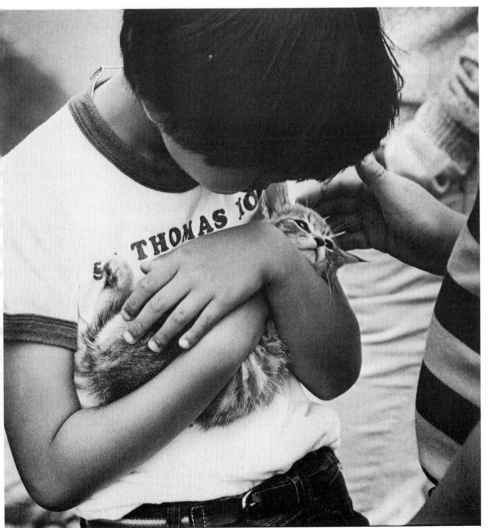

"And how do you think a rabbit should be picked up?" Nina asked.

One little boy in the fourth row held up his hand. "By the ears?" he asked.

"No you should never pick up rabbits by the ears—it is extremely painful for them and can permanently damage their ears," said Nina. She picked up the rabbit correctly and showed the child how to cradle it in his arms. "Some people pick up rabbits by the ears because it seems convenient, but it is cruel," she explained.

Nina talked for about thirty minutes, covering many important points about the responsible care and humane treatment of pets. She explained the need for leash laws and licensing. She let the audience ask questions. When the program was over, all the kids wanted to get a close look at the pets, so they filed across the stage and gave Snoopy and the others a quick pat before they went back to their classrooms.

SPCAs and humane societies across the country conduct humane education through schools and clubs, for children and adults. Often, tours of the shelters are given. Humane education directors publish magazines and hold seminars for school teachers, to alert them to the need for teaching children kindness to animals and to help them with printed materials and visual aids.

Some humane education directors make regular appearances on local radio and TV programs to talk about animal problems and animal care. Others have booths in shopping centers and give out humane education literature. As George Angell, Henry Bergh, Caroline Earle White and the other early humanitarians believed, education is an important way to change people's attitudes toward animals, and to help create a more humane world.

Schoolchildren are conducted on a tour of an animal shelter.

People who conduct humane education don't often get the satisfaction of seeing immediate results. It takes a very long time to change the attitudes of the public.

For example, men and women teaching education have been warning pet owners for years not to leave their animals in parked cars in warm weather, even with the windows open a crack. On an 85-degree day, the temperature in a car can rise to 120 degrees in ten minutes, even in the shade and with the car windows slightly open. SPCAs and humane societies continually remind the public of this through literature and speeches—yet, every year, hundreds of pets suffer and die of heat exhaustion in their owners' parked cars.

Humane education teachers have also warned people that cats fall out of open windows and get killed or badly hurt. Cats sitting on window ledges lose their balance and fall, or they get distracted by birds or insects and leap out before they think. Veterinarians are continually setting the broken bones of those cats that survive such falls; they call these accidents the "high-rise syndrome." And untold numbers of cats never live long enough to even be taken to a vet. Humane education teachers urge people to get screens, because cats can squeeze out of windows that are open just a few inches. Yet, to this day, most people believe that cats don't fall out of windows.

Nevertheless, humane education does have an effect. People seem to be more aware than they were a hundred years ago. If someone today suggested rounding up stray dogs and drowning them in the river or clubbing them to death, as was done in the nineteenth century, most people would not stand for it. Every year, new laws to protect animals are passed because of pressure from the public. There is no doubt that attitudes are changing, though slowly.

At the SPCA in our story, Tim was still shy with strangers, but he had become relaxed and trusting with Mrs. Hamilton, Bill, and the other shelter employees he saw regularly. He was a very sweet and appealing dog. Mrs. Hamilton felt sure the right person would come along who would want him, and she had resolved to give him every chance to be adopted.

One day Jody and her boyfriend Steve, who also volunteered at the shelter, gave Tim a bath.

"Come on, boy, don't be scared," Jody said, as she and Steve lifted the surprised dog into the tub. They handled him gently and spoke to him encouragingly the whole time they bathed, dried, and brushed him. Tim didn't struggle—in fact, it felt good.

A very curly dog in the cage next to him was taken out one day and returned with a fancy haircut. The SPCA ran a dog-grooming school at the shelter, taught by a professional to people who wanted to become dog groomers. Dogs from the shelter were chosen for demonstration and practice in the grooming classes. Some people coming to the shelter to adopt dogs preferred those with stylish haircuts, especially if the animals were purebred, like poodles or terriers. The grooming helped the dogs' chances for adoption.

One event in Tim's life was not as pleasant as his bath but certainly was not painful. He was led to Dr. Buckley's clinic and given an injection of anesthetic. As soon as he was sound asleep, he was subjected to the quick, simple neutering operation. When he woke up, he was a little groggy and uncomfortable. But by the next morning, he had forgotten all about it.

In recent years, SPCAs and humane societies around the United States have launched vigorous programs to encourage people to spay or neuter their pets. There are many advantages to this—for the animals, for pet owners, and for society in general.

The main advantage is that spaying and neutering reduce the number of surplus and homeless pets. At present, an estimated ten thousand cats and dogs are born every hour in the United States. While it's true that there are few things on earth as cute as kittens and puppies, people who allow their pets to breed should understand that by permitting more to be born, they are causing others to die.

Let's say a family has one female dog and one female cat, and each has a litter of eight. Those puppies and kittens grow up, and the females have litters. Their offspring also breed, and so on. If the original two pets and their female descendents all have two litters a year, within only four years there could easily be fifty thousand more dogs and cats in the world! People who want to observe the "miracle of birth" in their pets might think about this.

Since millions of homeless dogs and cats die of starvation and disease each year, and 10 million more are killed at shelters because they don't get adopted, doesn't it seem selfish and cruel to add to this problem? The situation is made worse by pet shops. Most buy their pets wholesale from factorylike places called "puppy mills" and "kitten mills," where dogs and cats are bred continually to produce merchandise in the form of puppies and kittens, so the owners of these mills and the pet shops can make money. Many of the young animals die being shipped to the cities where the pet shops are, and some die in the shops. Those that live are often sick. People who buy animals from pet shops should realize that they are keeping the puppy and kitten mills in business.

Spayed and neutered dogs and cats make much better pets. The males don't roam looking for females or get into fights and get hurt, as unneutered males do. Also, unneutered male cats tend to have a raunchy smell and to spray very smelly urine everyplace, making themselves less than delightful to have around, especially in the house. Neutered male cats in general don't do this. Neutering also reduces the chances of prostate cancer in older male cats.

As for females, the spayed animal doesn't have to endure regular periods of going into heat. Her owner doesn't have to listen to her cries or contend with her unwanted suitors who hang around. Female cats are uncomfortable during their heat periods, and unless they become pregnant, they howl a lot and sometimes neglect their litterbox training. Spaying prevents all this—and also makes the pet far less likely to develop cancer and infections of the reproductive system in her older years.

The neutering operation for male animals is called castration. It can be performed any time after he is six or seven months old and is a simple operation. The dog or cat is lightly anesthetized, and his testicles are removed through a tiny incision, He is usually on his feet and eating a meal a few hours later.

A female dog or cat can be spayed (not "spaded," as some people erroneously say) as soon as she is five or six months old. It's best not to have her spayed when she is in heat, and of course she should be in good health, for spaying is a more complicated operation than castration is for a male. The operation involves removing the ovaries and uterus— her reproductive apparatus. The animal will be walking around in less than twenty-four hours, but should be kept warm and quiet for a few days. She will have a little scar on her belly, and the stitches must be removed a week or ten days after the operation.

There are many mistaken notions about spaying and neutering, and it's a good idea for pet owners to know the facts. For instance, don't let anyone tell you that your pet will automatically get fat. While the animal may possibly have a greater tendency to put on weight, the owner can control this. Unless a pet knows how to open the refrigerator by itself, the owner can regulate its meals so that it eats just enough to maintain a healthy size and shape. The only thing that will make an animal fat is overeating combined with lack of exercise, not neutering or spaying.

Some people are reluctant because they feel they are depriving their pets of the pleasure of active sex lives and having babies. But these well-meaning people should not confuse a dog or cat's sexuality with human sexuality. The animals never realize they're missing anything. And in fact, there is no evidence that their mating is anything more than relieving a physical urge. When they are spayed or castrated, they no longer feel the urge.

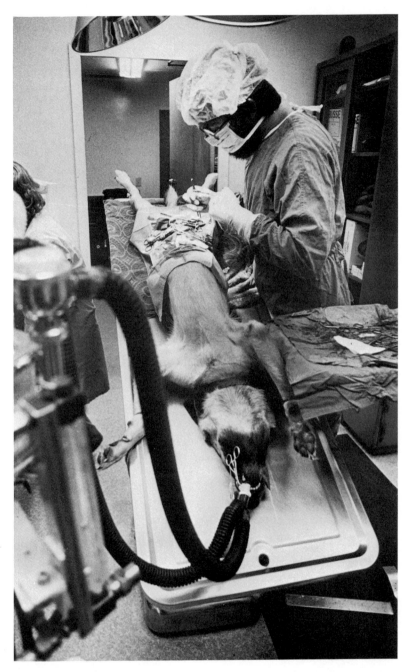

A female German shepherd–mixed breed undergoes a spay operation in the veterinary clinic of a modern animal shelter.

Another question that is raised is whether the operation will change a pet's personality. The only difference is that the animal will probably become more home-loving and affectionate and usually more fastidious about its hygiene.

It's true that because kittens and puppies are so enchanting, they usually stand a better chance of being adopted from animal shelters than older pets do. But of course, for every kitten and puppy that's adopted, many older cats and dogs are euthanized.

Nobody is suggesting that we create a world where there are no kittens and puppies at all. But many people hope that the time will come when there is a balance between wanted and unwanted pets. Then, there could be carefully regulated breeding so that there will be a home waiting for every kitten and puppy that is born. There would be no more euthanizing of healthy pets. The only animals that would be put to sleep in this ideal world would be those that are incurably injured or ill.

Because Tim was a full-grown dog, there was no need to wait for his operation. Mrs. Hamilton asked to have him castrated as soon as it became apparent that he would get over his fear and could be put up for adoption. Some good shelters automatically spay or neuter all their adult animals that are adoptable.

In the case of young puppies and kittens, the persons who adopt them are asked to pay a deposit toward the operation, as Princess Leia's adopters did. Then, when the pets are old enough, they are brought back to the shelter's clinic for the procedure. Shelters that don't have their own clinics make arrangements for private veterinarians to do it.

A vigilant shelter keeps a record of each puppy and kitten that is adopted and notes the month when it is due for spaying or neutering. Then, a volunteer or shelter employee telephones the owner with a reminder that the young dog or cat must be scheduled for the operation. Sometimes the owners refuse, or the pet has been given away or even has died. However, most people, when reminded, follow through, especially if they have already paid a deposit.

Some states or counties now require the neutering or spaying of pets adopted from shelters. Such laws are a good step in the direction of achieving the balance between wanted and unwanted pets.

Dr. Buckley also gave Tim his shots against distemper and rabies. Tim was now a neutered, vaccinated young dog with a shiny, clean coat. He was still a bit shy but growing bolder every day. Would just the right person come along and get him out of his cage, give him love and a good home?

Lost and Found

ONE DAY, SNOOPY WAS ADOPTED. It happened just like that—a couple came into the shelter with an eight-year-old boy who picked out Snoopy from among all the puppies. The parents filled out adoption forms and were interviewed by Mrs. Hamilton, who, after reviewing their forms, decided that they seemed like responsible people. They paid the adoption fee, signed a promise to bring Snoopy back to be neutered when he was old enough, and walked out with him in a cardboard carrying box.

In the car, the boy opened the box so that Snoopy could put his head out. He petted the excited puppy.

"Shall we keep his name—Snoopy—or should we change it?" he asked his parents.

"It's up to you, Mark," said the mother. "But since he already knows his name, it might be less confusing for him if you kept it."

Mark and his parents lived in an apartment house, so one of the first things he did was to take Snoopy around the block on his leash. Snoopy did not yet know how to walk properly on the leash, for he had only been out with Jody a few times, but he enjoyed the adventure. Mark praised him and cleaned up after him when he relieved himself at the curb. Then the boy played in his room with Snoopy until the exhausted pup fell asleep in his box beside Mark's bed.

These were a far different sort of people than Snoopy's first family. The parents were intelligent and kind, and they saw to it that Mark took good care of his dog. They understood the pup's needs and feelings. Snoopy had very few accidents in the house and was quiet when left alone. It looked like a bright future and a happy life for this little brown dog.

However, things don't always work out the way they should. In less than two weeks after Snoopy's arrival, the family received a notice from the landlord of the apartment building, telling them that pets weren't allowed, and that they would have to give up their dog or move.

Mark and his parents were devastated. They looked carefully at the lease for their apartment and finally saw, buried in very small print, a rule that forbade pets.

Mark's father telephoned the landlord. "Our son's dog does not create any disturbance," he said. "Our neighbors say they don't mind him at all. Why must we give him up?"

But his protest did no good whatsoever. The landlord did not care about individual tenants or about the justice of what he did—he made whatever rules he thought he could get away with under the housing laws. He even tried to enforce rules of his own that were illegal. Unfortunately, most no-pet rules are legal.

What sometimes happens in an apartment house is that there may be one tenant who allows his pet to create a nuisance. This one person may have a dog that barks all day when it's left alone, which disturbs other tenants. Or, perhaps the dog makes a mess in the halls of the building. Or, somebody may have a lot of cats and not take sufficient care of their litter boxes, so that a bad odor emanates from the apartment.

A building owner has a right to be angry in these individual situations, and there are plenty of provisions in standard leases and in the law that give a landlord the right to force such a tenant to be more considerate. The landlord can even evict people whose pets truly create problems.

But usually a landlord doesn't bother to deal with an offending tenant on an individual basis. He thinks it's too much trouble, so he decides: *No pets for anybody.* He puts a no-pet clause in the leases. And therefore, maybe fifty or more other people who have pets that are creating no problems at all are forced to give them up or find other places to live.

A building owner may even try to force out people who can't bear to part with their pets, just so he can get higher rents from new tenants that move in. And of course, if the prospective tenants have pets, they must give them up before they can rent the apartment or house.

In recent years, there has been very little new housing built, especially apartment buildings. Vacant apartments are extremely scarce. So in most cases, people cannot afford to give up their apartment—they would not be able to find another. Or, even if they found one, it would probably be in a building that also had a rule against pets. In cities all over the country, there is a terrible pressure against people having pets.

Because of this shortage of apartments, people are intimidated by landlords, and they don't realize that if they go to court, they can sometimes win and keep their pets. An increasing number of lawyers are becoming interested in taking cases involving the rights of pet owners. A family should never automatically give up a pet just because the landlord tells them to but should get legal advice and defend themselves if necessary. While the law seems to be all on the side of landlords, the courts are not.

People who don't like animals have no right to make rules that other people can't have them. However, pet owners should never allow their animals to bother other people. Dogs that run loose not only get into trouble but get hurt or killed. They sometimes dig up other people's gardens, tip over garbage cans, annoy or even kill other pets, and cause accidents by darting into the streets in the paths of cars. People should keep their dogs in fenced yards or walk them on leashes and clean up after them in the streets. It is not true that it's cruel to keep dogs under control. The animals adapt perfectly well and are far healthier and live much longer than those that are allowed to roam.

A dog that was allowed to run loose was hit by a car. When his owners heard what it would cost for medical care to heal his broken legs, they rejected him. The shelter veterinarian took care of him anyway, and when the dog recovered, he was adopted.

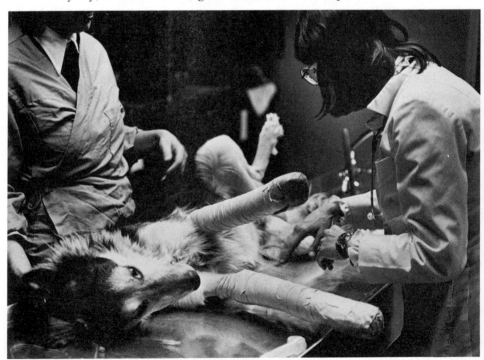

Cats are best kept indoors. Cats that are allowed to roam get hit by cars, and their famous curiosity causes them to get hurt, trapped, or lost. Some cats kill birds, which understandably bothers many people, even though the cats don't know they are doing anything wrong. Cats that are not neutered get into fights, howl at night, and keep neighbors awake. If more dog and cat owners behaved responsibly in caring for their pets, other people wouldn't have any complaints.

However, even those people who do everything right with their animals and don't allow them to annoy anyone else are not protected from injustice. That is what happened to Mark's family, and they assumed they had no choice but to give up Snoopy.

Of course, they did not abandon him. Although the adoption contract they had signed at the SPCA had stated that he should be returned to the shelter if they could not keep him, they found another home for him themselves. A man in the office where Mark's mother worked agreed to take Snoopy as a pet for his family. He picked up the puppy on his way home one evening.

Mark kissed Snoopy and ran to his room in tears. Mark's mother put the little dog in a cardboard carrying box. Snoopy, bewildered, felt himself placed in a car and the car move off. What was happening to him; where was he going?

On the way home, the man had to make a stop at a shopping center. He parked the car and left Snoopy in the box on the backseat.

If dogs could think as we do, Snoopy might have thought: This must be a mistake. I've got to get home to Mark. He fought his way out of the cardboard carrying box. Snoopy was now a half-grown, strong puppy. The car window by the driver's seat was partly open, so he wriggled out, fell to the

This dog's owner thinks his dog won't jump out of the car window and get lost, but like Snoopy, she could easily do so.

pavement, and took off. When the man came back to his car, he didn't even notice that the puppy was gone.

Snoopy found himself in the huge, lighted space. He dived under the nearest parked car when someone approached. He crouched there, trembling, as feet passed. Then he fled across the lot toward the highway.

He had no idea what direction to take—he just ran. Cars whizzing by frightened him, however, so he kept to the side of the road. That is what saved his life.

Bill was covering the front desk when the phone call came in. Someone reported finding an injured puppy. The person was telephoning from the other side of the city and had no means of transportation—could the shelter send an ambulance? Soon a driver was on the way.

"This dog looks familiar," the ambulance driver said as he placed the stretcher on a table in Dr. Buckley's clinic.

"Why, I think it's Snoopy!" exclaimed Mrs. Hamilton. At the sound of her voice, Snoopy opened his eyes, looked up at her, and thumped his tail a little. His hip hurt him badly.

Snoopy had wandered for three days without food or water or protection from the cold, always staying close to the highway which he must have thought would lead him to Mark. A car had pulled over onto the shoulder of the highway, and a man had gotten out to check one of his tires. Eagerly, trustingly, Snoopy had trotted up to him and tried to get in the car. Angrily, the man had given Snoopy a vicious kick that had sent him flying. When the dazed little dog had picked himself up, he discovered he could hardly walk. Pain shot through his hip and leg.

Dejected and miserable, Snoopy tried to continue. Finally, he could go no further, so he had just lain down by the roadside.

He had been almost unconscious when he felt himself lifted into a stretcher. He no longer cared what happened to him. And yet—now there was a voice he knew, speaking his name! There were familiar smells around him! He was too weak to respond much, but his whole being filled with joy.

Snoopy was X-rayed by Dr. Buckley's assistant. "It's a hairline fracture of the hip joint," said the veterinarian when she examined Snoopy and read the X ray. "He's a lucky dog. It will heal, and if the nerve regenerates—and it probably will—he won't even limp. All he needs is rest and quiet."

Snoopy was given food and water and placed in a cage in a quiet corner of the clinic. Everyone petted him. He was very glad to be there. Exhausted and happy, he fell asleep.

Karen Hamilton telephoned the family who had adopted Snoopy and heard why they had given him up. They had been greatly upset when the man from Mark's mother's office had reported that Snoopy had gotten out in the parking lot and been lost. Then Mrs. Hamilton telephoned the man who had lost Snoopy. He had been concerned about the puppy. When he had arrived home and discovered Snoopy was gone, he had driven back to the parking lot and searched for him. But because his children had been so disappointed not to get the dog they had been expecting, this man had adopted one for them through an ad in the newspaper.

Mrs. Hamilton was sorry that Mark could not keep Snoopy, but she was used to such happenings. The fact is that of all the dogs that are taken into homes from whatever sources, over a third of them are no longer in the same homes a year later. The turnover of pets, the casual transfer of dogs and cats from one home to another, is very high. Dr. Alan Beck, a scientist who has made studies of both dogs and dog ownership, says that surveys indicate that one puppy out of every three is given away by its owner before it is one year old. Any many of them end up in shelters. Millions of people change their minds or decide the pet is too much trouble. Or, they move into places where pets aren't allowed.

So Snoopy landed back at the SPCA and began to wait for a home all over again. Tim was still waiting, as were Luke Skywalker and Han Solo.

Little Yoda with the big ears had been lucky. Under Jody's care, he had put on weight and grown quite strong and healthy. When Jody's semester break was over and time came for her to start school again, she had planned to return Yoda to the shelter to be put up for adoption along with his two brothers.

However, Jody's boyfriend Steve had fallen in love with the little creature. He lived in the college dormitory and was not allowed to have a pet. But his mother, who lived in a neighboring town, loved cats. She already had three elderly and dignified cats of her own, but Steve took Yoda to visit her one day, tucked in the pocket of his jacket. When Yoda peeked out, his big ears and sweet face were too much for Steve's mother. So, over the grumbling of the older cats, Yoda was adopted on the spot. The big cats were not friendly to the kitten for a few days, but he learned not to pester them too much, and they grew to tolerate him within a week. Older cats, though they may be upset for a while if another grown cat is introduced into their household, will nearly always accept a kitten fairly soon. Steve's mother even came across one of the big cats washing Yoda with her tongue while the kitten purred contentedly.

12

Wild Animal Pets

As the man placed the big box on the front desk of the SPCA, what looked like a little black-gloved hand reached out through one of the holes in the side.

"It's our raccoon," said the man rather apologetically to Bill. "We have to give him up."

"Okay," said Bill, handing him a surrender form to fill out.

"We found him in the woods last spring when he was a baby," explained the man. "We left him for a couple of hours, thinking the mother might come back, but when we returned, he was still in the same spot, looking pitiful. He was obviously starving. So we brought him home and fed him with a bottle, and we've had him ever since. He was real cute and lived in the house till he got big. Then we built him a cage in the garage. Sometimes the kids walked him on a leash."

"Why are you giving him up?" asked Bill, though he could guess the answer.

"He isn't as tame anymore. He's bitten us a couple of times, and he has gotten out of his cage twice and wrecked the garage," replied the man. "We've thought of turning him loose, but I hear that once they've been raised in captivity, they might not survive on their own. Can you give him to a zoo?"

Bill opened the box carefully at one corner. The young raccoon looked up nervously and tried to climb out, standing up on his hind legs and scrabbling at the opening with his "hands." Bill quickly shut the box again to prevent the animal from escaping.

"His name is Oscar," commented the man. "So long, Oscar," he said to the box. "Behave yourself." He turned to Bill. "Please take good care of him."

Bill took Oscar back to a cage, where the animal began to pace back and forth, looking for an escape.

Oscar was not the only wild animal at the SPCA shelter. At that moment, there were also a snapping turtle, a horned owl, and a handsome, wild spotted cat called an ocelot, a native of Central America. All had been raised from infancy by people, and they were at the SPCA because they did not make good pets.

People often find orphaned or injured wild animals, in the woods or mountains or along the seacoast, and take them home to try to help them. What kind-hearted person could leave a helpless, little orphaned animal, crying for its mother, or an injured animal that will surely die of its wounds, starve, or fall prey to others? Unfortunately, the majority of the infants probably do not survive, since human beings can rarely replace the mothers. However, some live, and some of the injured animals heal. They become tame. The temptation to keep them as pets is strong.

Sooner or later, problems arise. People invariably find

that their cute baby raccoon, possum, fox, or squirrel has grown into a destructive and possibly unfriendly animal.

Virtually all animals are tame when they are infants and can be handled and cuddled. But as they grow up, something happens. Their instinctual programming takes over. While a dog or cat, or even a farm animal, will become *more* tame and friendly to human beings as it matures, provided it is well treated, just the opposite happens with a wild animal. Like Oscar, it will become *less* tame and friendly, no matter how well it is treated.

That's usually when these animals end up in shelters.

This little animal, a ferret, was owned by someone who thought it would be fun to have an unusual pet. When the animal turned out to be an unsuitable house pet, the owner then dumped her in an animal shelter.

The problem is that a wild animal that has been raised as a pet can't simply be released into its natural habitat. Its instinctual equipment has not been developed, and it has not learned a whole repertoire of complex skills from its parents. Wild animals are not necessarily born knowing how to find food and shelter and avoid danger—they must be taught. And any wild animal that has lived as a pet has lost its most basic and essential survival tool: fear of human beings.

If Oscar were merely taken out to the countryside and turned loose, he would soon get into trouble. He wouldn't know how to forage for food for himself and would starve to death. Or, he would seek out human habitation, looking for food. He would raid someone's garbage can and perhaps get shot or trapped. He might be killed by dogs. If people discovered he was tame, they might try to keep him as a pet until he bit someone or destroyed something, just as he had done before, and the pattern would be repeated.

By far, the best hope for an orphaned or injured wild animal is either a wildlife rescue and rehabilitation center or a private wildlife refuge, where knowledgeable people who have had a great deal of experience with native wild animals know how to treat them and release them safely.

A rescue and rehabilitation center is a place where injured, sick, or orphaned wild animals are confined and treated by caring people—usually professional biologists and perhaps other scientists—until the animals can be returned to the wild. These places must be licensed by the state. Private refuges are tracts of wilderness owned by people who encourage and protect the natural ecosystem, including the animals that are a part of it. These people may not be scientists but are naturalists who know a great deal about the trees, plants, birds, animals, and other living things on their land. Unfortunately, hunters and trappers often trespass into private refuges and kill animals anyway.

There are few places left where wild animals are truly safe from people, but these centers and refuges offer them a chance.

How do you find one of these places? That is a good question. Most people immediately call their state conservation, fish and game, or wildlife agency (the titles vary somewhat from state to state). Sometimes these state officers are sympathetic and will direct you to a rehabilitation center or a private refuge. However, you should be warned of several factors.

One is that because it is illegal to take an animal from the wild in the first place, you might get into trouble for your Good Samaritan act. State officials might slap a fine on you. Some will simply recommend killing the animal. And it's a good idea to remember that these government agencies get their income from selling hunting, fishing, and trapping licenses. Their interests lie with people who are involved in these activities; they work closely with these "sportsmen's" groups. Some state agencies even maintain game farms where they raise game birds to stock the woods for hunters to shoot. So especially if you are trying to help a game animal such as a deer or a pheasant, there is no point in saving its life only to set it free where it will become a target for hunters.

Life is never easy for wild animals, even if they are relatively undisturbed in their natural habitat. They must continually struggle to find food and to avoid being eaten by other animals that prey on them for food. They must endure injuries, sickness, accidents, and harsh weather. They must survive in increasingly polluted air, water, and land. They must avoid being shot, poisoned, or trapped by people.

In many areas of our country, wild animals are under continual pressure from the spread of human habitation. Towns, shopping centers, and industrial plants are taking

A sea lion pup, found abandoned on a beach and rescued by the California Marine Mammal Center, must be force-fed or he will die.

This sea lion pup, also abandoned, gets a drink of water at the California Marine Mammal Center. She will be released into the ocean when old enough to be on her own.

over the land where wild animals live. As our woods and lakes are populated or polluted, these animals find it increasingly difficult to survive. Hunting and trapping take their toll, but loss of habitat is also a major reason many species are disappearing.

Nevertheless, when you are confronted with a wild animal that truly needs help, you have to do your best for it, no matter how difficult. It deserves a chance to live. An animal protection organization or an animal shelter can often direct you to wildlife rescue and rehabilitation centers or to private wildlife refuges.

Other wild animals known as "exotics" also have a sad history as pets for human beings. Some folks cannot resist buying these creatures from wild animal dealers. The word *exotic* applies to animals such as monkeys, jaguars, boa constrictors, and the like, that are not native to this country. Or, it may apply to an animal that is foreign to the place where it finds itself—a bobcat or bear in a city, for example. Even though bobcats and bears are native to some parts of the United States, they are certainly exotic in cities.

It's amazing what exotic animals people try to keep as pets, from lions to tarantulas, even though it may be against the law to import most of them, keep them in cities, or to take them from the wild. And sooner or later, these animals turn out to be unsatisfactory, destructive, maybe dangerous.

People learn that the lively monkey they thought would be such an adorable pet in fact bites and can totally demolish a room in a matter of minutes. And every so often, an exotic creature that's kept as a pet seriously hurts or kills someone.

As soon as an exotic pet becomes too much of a nuisance, or dangerous, it usually ends up—where else?—in an animal shelter. Just as dog and cat owners believe that a shelter can always find homes for their unwanted pets, they fantasize that a shelter can find homes for their exotic pets in zoos.

A boa constrictor, an illegal and possibly dangerous pet, was confiscated by authorities and brought to a shelter.

Zoos rarely want or need these animals. Wildlife rehabilitation centers and private wildlife refuges can only take native species that can be helped to survive in the available wilderness. An exotic animal can only exist on its own in a climate and ecosystem similar to its natural habitat. For example, a little monkey whose habitat is an equatorial jungle could not be released into the woods of New England. So for the most part, exotic pets must be euthanized.

The ocelot at the SPCA in our story paced its cage endlessly. The owl had withdrawn into a depressed sort of stupor. Oscar fiddled with the latch on his cage door, sniffed the air, and appeared totally bewildered and upset. Mrs. Hamilton looked at them sympathetically. Just as the dogs and cats did not belong in cages in the SPCA, neither did they.

About two hours' drive from the SPCA there was a private wildlife refuge. The owners, Clark and Dorothy Perry, had had much experience saving and rehabilitating wild mammals and birds. They had helped out Mrs. Hamilton before. She telephoned them.

"What have you got this time, Karen?" asked Dorothy Perry.

"A young adult raccoon named Oscar, a snapping turtle, and a huge horned owl," replied Mrs. Hamilton. "We also have an ocelot. I know you can't take him, but do you have room for the others?"

"No problem," replied Dorothy. "We have a fairly large raccoon colony on our land, and many of them come to the house regularly to be fed. They might not accept Oscar right away, but we'll set him free gradually, and he will know he can always count on us for dinner. The turtle we'll simply release by the lake when warm weather comes. But the owl— can it fly? We may have to teach it to hunt for food. Anyway, we'll take it and work out some solution for it that makes it happier than it probably is at the shelter."

"We would greatly appreciate your help," said Karen Hamilton. "Have you had many trappers sneaking onto your land and setting traps this winter?"

"Oh, yes, we've found several traps and confiscated them before they caught any animals, but we have to patrol our woods continually," sighed Dorothy. "It's the same every year. Even though our property is posted with No Hunting, No Fishing, No Trapping signs, those people come in anyhow. Autumn with the hunters is even worse. When we catch them on our land and ask them to leave, they can become very ugly. They act as though we have no right to prevent them from shooting birds and animals on our property. They sometimes threaten us. I worry about our wildlife, our pets, and even about our own lives."

"It's an outrage," exclaimed the shelter director. "Won't your local sheriffs do anything about it?"

"Oh, they promise to, but there's little they can do. They don't seem too anxious anyhow—most of them are hunters or trappers themselves, so they sympathize with their buddies," Dorothy Perry explained.

"Well, Oscar is still better off at your refuge than anywhere else I know of," said Mrs. Hamilton. "We'll send the three animals up to you next Saturday. Thanks so much, Dorothy."

Jody and Steve volunteered to drive Oscar, the turtle, and the owl up to the Perrys' in Steve's van. And so, thanks to the generosity of two wildlife lovers who knew a great deal about them and were fortunate to have a large piece of land, three wild creatures were given a chance for life.

The beautiful spotted cat from Central America would have to live with someone who had an appropriately large enclosure in the right climate and knew how to care for such an exotic animal. Mrs. Hamilton had sent out inquiries all over the country; perhaps an answer would come soon in the form of a good home for the muscular, energetic, handsome wild animal. Otherwise, it would be more humane to euthanize him than to keep him indefinitely caged at the SPCA.

"And soon it will be Easter again, and we'll probably get some rabbits, ducklings, and baby chicks," Bill reminded Mrs. Hamilton.

In the days and weeks following Easter, animal shelters across the United States must accept the casualties of the season. Some people think it is cute to give children these living creatures as Easter toys. Large numbers of them die from too much handling and improper care; some survive to be dumped in the local shelter.

Fortunately, the practice of giving live animals to little kids as Easter presents is declining.

"Remember, we only had a few last year," Mrs. Hamilton said to Bill. "Cheer up. I think we're making headway with the Easter bunny syndrome."

13

Pets as
Laboratory Tools

"THERE'S A GUY at the front desk who wants to adopt some dogs," said Bill quietly, coming into Karen Hamilton's office. "I'm conducting a routine adoption interview, but there's something fishy about him that I can't quite get a handle on. For one thing, he wants four dogs. Medium-sized to large. Says he has a big, fenced yard. According to him, his last dog died of old age. Somehow I don't believe anything he's telling me. What should I do?"

"Stall him," advised Mrs. Hamilton. "Keep asking questions, and if you still feel uneasy about him, just thank him for coming in, take his name, address, and telephone number, and tell him we'll call him as soon as we have the sort of dogs he wants. Then we can try to check him out."

In a few minutes, she could hear the man's angry voice clear down the hall to her office. As he left the shelter, she peeked through the blinds at her window and caught a glimpse of him as he walked, scowling, to his car. He looked familiar.

127

She went back to work, but her mind strayed to a scene, four years earlier, when the City Council was holding public hearings on a law called Pound Seizure.

A Pound Seizure law *requires* pounds and shelters that receive any public funds to turn over unclaimed dogs and cats to medical laboratories to be used in experimentation. Such a law exists in several cities and states. Most states do not have statewide Pound Seizure laws, but on the other hand they don't *prohibit* the sale of animals to laboratories. A local or private shelter can sell animals to a laboratory if it chooses to.

Therefore, a dog or cat that is picked up or surrendered to a pound, or to a shelter that functions as the pound, can end up as an experimental tool in a laboratory. The Humane Society of the United States estimates that as many as 262,000 dogs and cats from shelters are used in research every year. Dealers who get the pets from the shelters, and researchers and laboratory workers as well, prefer gentle, easily handled animals—like Snoopy, for example.

Animal lovers everywhere despair at the distress and pain that research animals of all kinds very often endure. The Animal Welfare Act, which was passed to protect laboratory animals, does say that research animals must be transported, housed, and maintained humanely. But it is, in general, carelessly observed and poorly enforced. And it says nothing about the types of experiments the animals are used in, even experiments that cause them great and prolonged suffering.

Researchers who perform experiments on animals insist that this work is necessary in order to learn about human and animal diseases and discover cures. People who agree with their point of view say that most pound animals are going to be euthanized anyway, so why not let them be useful in the cause of science before they die? Scientists are especially quick to emphasize the role that animals play in cancer research, because cancer is such a terrible and dreaded disease that most people agree that any sacrifice of animals is worth it in a search for cures.

However, the fact is that cancer research is only a very tiny percentage of the research using animals. In other experiments, millions of animals are burned, blinded, and battered; they are exposed to radiation; they are forced to smoke cigarettes and become addicted to many types of drugs. Transplants and amputations are performed on them. Animals are even made to suffer and die to test the safety of new cosmetics and household products such as detergents and cleansers.

Psychological research can cause as much fear and pain as the worst physical experiments. In these studies, animals are given electric shocks to make them perform in certain ways so that scientists can observe them. Animals are confined so they cannot move; they are forced to attack each other; they are deprived of food, sleep, or companionship; baby animals are separated from their mothers and confined in isolation—all in the name of learning about *human* nature. Many scientists, however, don't believe that the behavior of frightened, depressed, deprived, and severely stressed captive animals tells us much about human behavior.

Most of us do agree that cures for diseases must be found, that better surgical procedures should be developed, and that products and medicines should be tested for safety. People have a right to medical knowledge and to safe medicines and treatments. The use of animals in this regard is a complicated issue. Our right to make animals suffer in research is a serious moral and ethical question. Many people say we do not have this right.

On the practical side, animal research is not always trustworthy, because chemicals may turn out to affect humans differently than the way they tested out on animals. There is

Laboratory researchers opened this cat's head, planted electrodes in her brain, and bolted a metal plate to her skull. In an experiment, the researchers can attach electric wires to the metal plate and give the cat painful shocks to the brain. *Courtesy of Henry Spira*

reason to hope that better methods and tools of research can be developed to replace many of the experiments in which some 70 to 80 million animals, including mice, rats, rabbits, primates, and other animals, as well as dogs and cats, now die every year. There is reason to believe that some particularly cruel experiments will be simply stopped, without putting the human race in danger.

Alternatives to animals already exist for some kinds of research, and others are slowly being developed. Cell cultures, tissue, bacteria, computers, and other technologies can be substituted for some animal experiments and are cheaper, quicker, and more reliable. Under pressure from animal welfare groups, a few companies that use animals to test and develop their products have given money to scientists to develop alternatives. And bills have been introduced in Congress that would set aside some government research money to pay scientists to work on discovering reliable substitutes for living animals wherever possible.

Millions of dollars, however, are spent by our government and by private companies on research that uses animals. Unfortunately, when scientists earn their living by doing research with animals, they don't feel the urge to change and use substitutes, even when they are available. Animals are the traditional tools of research, and since there are no laws against it, most scientists go on using them.

Whether or not experimentation on animals is justified, the question involving pounds and SPCAs is much simpler: Should they be forced or permitted to supply dogs and cats for it? The vast majority of shelter animals have been pets— should they end up in laboratories?

What does the public think is the central purpose of a shelter? If people decide that pounds and shelters should serve as refuges for lost and abandoned pets, then these animals should not be doomed to medical research. In many places, the public has already indicated that it wants its tax money and donations to be spent on providing practical and decent protection for stray and unwanted dogs and cats. People have determined that the purpose of their pound, SPCA, or humane society is to return lost pets to their owners, protect animals against cruelty, shelter those that are homeless, and offer pets for adoption—but not to service the medical schools and experimental laboratories with living research tools.

Dogs and cats that have been pets are often so frightened, upset, or depressed when they find themselves in laboratory cages and subjected to experiments that they become sick. Some die even before they are used in experiments. Their body chemistry may be so changed by their fear and depression that the results of the tests on them are unreliable. Also, their genetic, hereditary background is unknown.

Even in communities where Pound Seizure laws exist, some shelters refuse to give up their animals. Often, this is how Pound Seizure laws come to the attention of the public. The first news people have that such an ordinance exists in their town may come about as a result of publicity about a shelter's refusal to surrender its animals. Then, if enough people complain, public hearings are held about it in the legislature and sometimes the laws are repealed.

At times, the opposite happens. In places where the sale of shelter pets is permitted, a callous shelter director may regard this as a good way to make money and may sell pets to laboratories as a source of income. If one city permits this in a state where most of the other cities have passed ordinances against it, you can be sure that the pound in that city will do a booming business selling pets to research laboratories all over the state. If the shelter director is greedy, he or she may even hustle pets off to laboratories before owners have a chance to reclaim them.

In a few states, it is now against the law for shelters and pounds to sell animals to labs. Yet, dishonest persons may get animals from shelters under the pretense of adopting them as pets—and then secretly sell them to the labs to make money. Unfortunately, laboratories may not be too particular or ask questions about where the animals come from.

Karen Hamilton remembered the hearings in the City Council very well. She had testified against the Pound Seizure law, and everyone in the SPCA had celebrated when the law was repealed.

She walked out to the front desk. "Bill, I'm sure that man was at the City Council committee hearings on the Pound Seizure law," she said. "He was seated in the committee room with the fellow who used to come here and try to collect animals from us, and who testified in favor of the law. The two men were whispering together throughout the hearings. I got the impression they both did the same kind of work—collecting animals for research laboratories."

"That's it!" exclaimed Bill. "The medical laboratories can't get animals from pounds anymore, so creeps like him come around. I bet this guy has a deal with some small medical school somewhere in the state that doesn't want to pay the price of dogs from a regular research animal breeder. He adopts dogs from shelters and then sells them to the medical school at prices below the breeders' prices, but still makes a profit for himself."

"You could be right," said Mrs. Hamilton. "This fellow never came here himself to try to collect animals, so he thinks none of us would recognize him. Did you get his name, Bill? I want to warn all the other shelters. Somebody might unknowingly let him adopt dogs."

"He gave a name, but it might not be his real one," Bill pointed out.

"Well, I'll describe him, too," the director answered. "I'm sure none of the shelters in this part of the state would want to let someone adopt dogs and turn them over to a lab."

Pet owners everywhere should be aware that people like this man really exist and will kidnap pets. If such a person finds a dog running loose, or tied in front of a store or restaurant, or even alone in a yard, he or she will just walk off with it. The most trusting, friendly pets are the most likely targets.

Adopted!

THE NEXT PEOPLE who came into the SPCA wanted to adopt two young kittens. They seemed like suitable pet owners. They were a young couple who lived in their own house, not in an apartment where pets might not be allowed. They were both employed and financially able to take care of pets. They did not hesitate to agree to neutering.

They had had cats before, and in fact now had one older cat. The woman told Bill that she had once had a cat that had lived to be twenty-one; it had been adopted as a kitten and had stayed in the family all its life. These were all points in the couple's favor. Bill felt satisfied that they would be responsible pet owners.

The couple chose Luke Skywalker and Han Solo, who were nearly four months old and were lively and beguiling.

When they arrived at their new home, the two kittens explored it eagerly. They were polite to the older cat, who regarded them with distaste and retreated to the top of a cabinet where she could watch from a distance.

A day or two after they adopted Luke and Han, the young couple went away for the afternoon. The weather was bright and sunny, unusually warm for the season.

"The cats are all out in the yard. Shouldn't we put the kittens in the house?" they asked each other before they left. "Oh, they'll be all right. They're having such a good time, let's leave them out," they decided. So off they went.

Luke and Han were chasing each other in the yard, enjoying their freedom, while the older cat gazed at them, still disapprovingly. As the day passed, the kittens found more objects to play with. They were having the time of their lives.

Suddenly, from around the house came three large dogs. Luke and Han stopped in their tracks, arched their backs, and fluffed up their tails as the dogs bore down on them. Too late, they realized these creatures were not like the puppies they had been with in the pet therapy trips to the nursing homes and hospitals. As the dogs barked and wheeled around them, the kittens ran for the house. But the doors were closed. In panic, they raced for any shelter they could find. The dogs barked and chased them, trampling plants and knocking over flowerpots and garden furniture. The larger cat had fled up a tree to safety at the first sight of the dogs; the inexperienced kittens simply ran this way and that.

Suddenly one of the dogs caught Han Solo and tossed him in the air, then picked him up and shook him. Han gave out one pitiful shriek, then he was still. His neck had been broken.

Luke Skywalker, backed under a thick bush, watched as his brother's body was tossed playfully about by the dogs. One of them sniffed at Luke but apparently decided it was too much trouble to scramble under the thorny bush to capture the second kitten. After a while, the dogs ran off, one of them still carrying the limp body of Han in his mouth.

For hours, Luke stayed under the bush. The afternoon wore on, and it became chilly. The kitten had never been outdoors so long. He became cold and frightened, and he missed his brother.

He cried at the door of the house, but of course no one came. Then he crept fearfully down the driveway toward the house across the street. Maybe someone would let him in there, he thought. He never made it—a car came too fast. Luke's body was crushed in the road.

When the young couple came home, they noticed their neighbor's three big dogs playing in the road, but it was beginning to get dark so they didn't see anything else. They were very upset when they found one kitten dead in the road and the other missing. They began to look everywhere for Han Solo.

After a search, the young man found his body in the driveway of the neighbor who owned the three dogs. Holding Han in his hands, he rang the bell of the house.

"Your dogs killed our kitten," he said simply to the man who came to the door, his dogs trotting beside him.

The man stared at Han's body and didn't seem to know what to say.

"What is it?" asked the man's wife as she and two children came to the door, too. "Oh, my God," she exclaimed as she saw the kitten. "Come here, children, don't look." She made a face as though she was smelling something bad and acted as if the kitten's body was some horrible object that might infect the children.

"That's funny—our dogs haven't been out of the house all day," lied the man.

The children looked at their father in surprise but didn't say anything.

"But we saw your dogs in the road when we came home a

little while ago," said the young man. "And I found our kitten's body just now in your driveway."

The owner of the dogs was silent. His wife said nothing also and looked very hostile. The children were taking in the scene. What were they learning from all this, the young man wondered.

He turned to go. "You know, there's a leash law here that says dogs must be leashed outdoors," he said. "Don't let your dogs run loose again or I'll file a complaint with the authorities."

When the young couple turned up at the SPCA to adopt two more kittens, Bill questioned them at length. At first they wouldn't say much about what had happened, but Bill persisted and got the full story out of them. He was sickened.

"I'm sorry, but we don't have any more kittens," said Bill. It was true at that moment. But even if the shelter had been full of kittens, Bill would have found some excuse not to let these people have two more. They probably would take better care of their cats from now on, but Bill felt that animals should not be so easily replaced—like broken toys.

"Don't feel so bad. How could you have known?" said Karen Hamilton later, trying to comfort Bill, though she felt as bad as he did. "They seemed like good pet owners. We can't foresee everything that can happen, and there is just no way we can predict that people will always behave responsibly."

There are two general points of view about giving animals out for adoption, and shelters tend to lean toward one or the other.

One philosophy is that every animal deserves a chance for life, and that if a shelter holds out for perfect homes for its pets, few would be adopted. People at these shelters won't

let an animal go into an obviously unsuitable home. For example, they won't let someone adopt who looks like a drug
addict or wants an attack dog. But they don't have extremely
fussy adoption rules, and they try to get as many dogs and
cats as possible into homes. Adopters must fill out application forms and promise to take good care of the animals, but
there isn't much red tape and virtually no follow-up after-
ward to see how the adoption is working out.

Other, equally compassionate shelter workers believe

A girl has come with her family to adopt a cat.

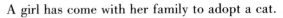

that extreme caution must be taken in allowing a pet to be adopted. These people see the atrocity cases that are brought in, the result of terrible human cruelty. They see the animals that have been abandoned by owners. These shelter people feel that unless an animal can be guaranteed a good home, it is better off dead. Because they are so careful about letting their pets out, they say, fewer are returned.

There's a lot to be said in favor of both points of view.

Bill was still thinking about Luke and Han as he went

A kitten, last of a litter, waits alone.

"I'll take this one."

The forms are filled out, donation paid—the kitten is hers.

about his work at the desk, when a man came in and asked to adopt a dog.

"What sort of dog do you want?" asked Bill, looking the man over carefully. The man was sloppily dressed but had a very nice, gentle way about him.

The man hesitated. "Well, I'm not particular what kind. I just want one for company," he said uncertainly. "I live alone."

Adopted! Here's one kitten that won't die in a shelter.

"Can you have dogs where you live?" Bill wanted to know.

"Well, there's nothing in my lease against it, and half the families in my building have dogs, so it must be okay," the man answered. "I think I'd like a medium-sized, sort of doggy dog, nothing fancy."

Bill led him back to the kennel room. The man walked thoughtfully up and down the aisles, looking at each dog. He came to Tim's cage. Tim didn't move from his corner. The man and the dog gazed at each other for several minutes.

The man turned to Bill. "How about him?"

Now Bill hesitated. "This dog is quite shy. When he was brought in a few weeks ago, he had apparently been abused. He's come a long way toward warming up, but he still needs a lot of reassurance," he told the man. "Maybe you'd prefer a more outgoing dog."

"I'll take him," said the man. "I'm shy, too. We can reassure each other."

The man, whose name was John, filled out the adoption forms, patting Tim and speaking softly to him all the while. Bill watched, wondering if he was doing the right thing. When John got up to leave with Tim on a leash, the dog held back and seemed afraid.

"Come on, boy, let's go home," said his new owner, and he simply picked up his dog and walked out. John was slightly built and not very tall; Tim had put on weight and was not a small dog. The two looked very funny, the slender man carrying the big armful of a dog. Bill smiled in spite of himself. He made a mental note to telephone the next day to see how this adoption was progressing.

John hailed a taxi and got into it, still clutching Tim, who was trying to get away and run back to the shelter. The dog panted nervously all the way in the taxi ride. At his new owner's apartment, he retreated behind the couch. John let him stay there and simply gave him a bowl of water. A few hours later, he put food for the dog in back of the couch, but Tim would not eat.

John let Tim stay behind the couch all night, although he got up once or twice to look at him and speak to him reassuringly.

The next day he said good morning to Tim, patted him on the head, and went on into his kitchen. As he was drinking his coffee, he looked up to see Tim standing in the doorway. He had let the dog come to him when the animal himself felt ready. It was the beginning of a very close friendship.

For a long time, Tim couldn't seem to trust his luck. When John went out, the dog drooped; his eyes were sad, and he waited anxiously for his owner's return. When John took him out for walks, the dog hid behind his legs if anyone stopped to talk to them. John kept in touch with Bill at the SPCA and reported on Tim's progress. But it was clear that the timid dog at last had an owner he adored, and who loved him greatly.

Snoopy was still waiting. He had grown—he was still a puppy but was no longer the cuddly baby he had been when he was brought to the SPCA by his first family. When he went on pet therapy visits now, he went on a leash, not in a carrying cage. He still sometimes climbed into an elderly person's or a child's lap, but he was an armful.

One evening when he was on a routine pet therapy visit to a hospital with Nina, a crew from the local TV station was there to film the event. About thirty children were gathered around while Nina and the volunteers passed the tiny puppies and kittens from lap to lap. Snoopy was enjoying himself—he loved being out of his cage and free to romp about and be petted. He bounced around, licking a hand here, playfully tugging at a bathrobe there.

The producer of the television program was a young

woman who kept watching Snoopy as he played. "Paul, please get a lot of footage of that dog," she asked one of the cameramen. "He has so much personality—look how the children all respond to him!"

Snoopy was clearly the star of the show that evening, and the more attention he got, the more excited he became. People were laughing at him, and he loved it.

"This is great," said one of the crew members. "We're getting some wonderful stuff, especially of that little mutt."

Finally the evening was over, and the television crew was getting ready to leave. Nina and the volunteers began to gather the puppies and kittens into their carrying cages. One kitten was missing.

"Has anybody seen a black kitten?" asked Nina. She turned to one of the nurses. "Could it have gotten out of the room?"

Everybody looked everywhere for the missing kitten. Snoopy was standing with a volunteer who had him on a leash. Suddenly, Snoopy broke away, raced to a little girl in a wheelchair, and put his paws in her lap, wagging his tail and sniffing at the blanket she had tucked around her.

A light went on in Nina's head. She went over to the child. "Have you seen a black kitten?" she asked.

"Kitten? What kitten?" replied the girl innocently, but with a little smile.

Nina lifted the corner of the blanket from her lap. There, of course, was the tiny black kitten. Everyone in the room burst out laughing.

"Snoopy, you're a smart dog," said the television producer, crouching down and holding out her hand to Snoopy. "Come here and let me pet you." The puppy looked at her, raced across the room, and flung himself into her arms, almost knocking her off her feet. Slurp—he gave her a kiss.

"It's been a long time since I had a dog," said the young

woman. "Maybe I need one." Snoopy, sensing her reaction to him, wriggled with joy and kissed her face some more. "But I'm gone all day and sometimes in the evening," she said to Nina, who was waiting nearby.

"Well, why don't you adopt *two* pets," said Nina encouragingly. "Then they can keep each other company and won't be lonely the way a single animal is when its owner is out."

"You know, that's a good idea," said the television producer. "Let me think about it overnight." Snoopy whimpered when he was taken from her arms. "I'll come and get you tomorrow," she whispered in his ear.

She kept her word. The next day when Mrs. Hamilton appeared at his cage with the young woman and opened the door, Snoopy could hardly believe his eyes at first. He became hysterical with joy, leaping as high as he could, wagging not just his tail but his whole back end.

"And not only that, Snoopy," said Karen Hamilton. "You are going to have your very own cat to keep you company!" She was holding the little black kitten that had been hidden under the blanket. Slurp—Snoopy kissed the kitten, too, who sneezed and then began to purr.

The television producer was thrilled with her new pets. She filled out the adoption forms, paid the adoption fees, and paid a fee toward having both animals neutered when they were old enough. She gathered up booklets on cat and dog care. She had arranged for a reliable teenage neighbor to walk Snoopy whenever she had to work late. She bought Snoopy a bright red leash, put the kitten in a carrying box, and went out looking happy. Mrs. Hamilton and Bill and everyone else at the SPCA felt good about this adoption.

Snoopy never even looked back.

Other cats and dogs, in shelters all over the United States, are still waiting.

Will this dog go to a home or to the euthanasia room?

Further Information

BOOKS

Angel in Top Hat, by Zulma Steele, Harper & Bros., 1942.

In Defense of Animals, by J. J. McCoy, Seabury Press, 1978.

Men, Beasts, and Gods: A History of Cruelty and Kindness to Animals, by Gerald Carson, Scribner's, 1972.

Ordeal of the Animals, by Mel Morse, Prentice-Hall, 1968.

Reckoning with the Beast: Animals, Pain, and Humanity in the Victorian Mind, by James Turner, Johns Hopkins University, 1980.

Too Few Happy Endings: The Dilemma of the Humane Societies, by Margaret Poynter, Atheneum, 1981.

FILMS AND SLIDE SHOWS

The Animals Are Crying (documentary film, 30 mins., color/sound, 16 mm.). Unwanted dogs and cats and the daily life of an animal shelter. Available from the Humane

Society of the United States, 2100 L St. NW, Washington, D.C. 20037 (rental: $15).

The Family Chooses a Pet (film, 13 mins., color/sound, 16 mm.). How to select a suitable pet. May be borrowed from the Latham Foundation, Clement and Schiller, Alameda, California 94501 (handling/shipping: $10 if prepaid, $15 if billed). Or, may be purchased, $220, from Aims Instructional Media Services, Inc., 626 Justin Ave., Glendale, California 91201.

The History of the Humane Movement (slide show, about 40 color slides). Traces humans' relationships with animals from earliest known times to founding of nineteenth-century humane societies. Can be borrowed from the American Humane Education Society, Box 2244, Salem End Road, Framingham Center, Massachusetts 01701 (free except for shipping charges).

Home Is Belonging to Someone (filmstrip, 13 mins., color, sound cassette, 35 mm.). An abandoned dog ends up in an animal shelter. Available from the Boulder County Humane Society, 2323 55th St., Boulder, Colorado 80301 (purchase: $20, postage included).

PAWS (documentary film, 10 mins., color/sound, 16mm.). The fate of unwanted pets: euthanasia in a shelter. Available from Progressive Animal Welfare Society, Box 1037, Lynnwood, Washington 98036 (purchase: $50).

Who Cares, Anyway? (documentary film, 26 mins., color/sound, 16 mm.). The present overpopulation of pets and possible solutions. Available from Kinetic Film Enterprises Ltd., 781 Gerrard St. East, Toronto, Ontario M4M 1Y5 (rental: $75; purchase: $495).

A World to Build (documentary film, 18 mins., color/sound, 16 mm.). The work of the Animal Rescue League of Boston. May be borrowed from the Latham Foundation,

Clement and Schiller, Alameda, California 94501 (handling/shipping: $10 if prepaid, $15 if billed). Or, may be purchased, $235, from the Animal Rescue League of Boston, P.O. Box 265, Boston, Massachusetts 02117.

Note: An informative loose-leaf manual, *Films for Humane Education,* is a valuable aid to librarians, teachers, and group leaders. Gives all pertinent details on over a hundred films on animals, including many on pets and shelters. $4.75 plus $1 postage/handling. Argus Archives, 228 East 49 St., New York, New York 10017.

Sources and References

IN DOING THE RESEARCH for this book, I have learned from my visits to over twenty animal shelters in all parts of the United States; from my interviews with the directors and other staff members of many shelters; and from reading shelter magazines and newsletters, books, research papers, and special publications.

Here, I have tried to pinpoint as accurately as possible the sources of my information for each chapter. These references, plus the books and visual material listed under Further Information, should serve as a guide to anyone who wishes to explore specific subjects.

CHAPTERS 1 AND 2: "The Animal Shelter"
and "Thrown-Away Pets"

Animal Rescue League of Western Pennsylvania, Pittsburgh; ASPCA, New York; Humane Society of the United States, Washington, D.C.; Gretchen Scanlan, founder and former director, Kent Animal Shelter.

"Do You Know Where Your Dog Is?" by Anne Fadiman, *Life*, Sept. 1980.

"Pet Abandonment: Trashing the Human/Companion Animal Bond," by Alice A. DeGroot, D.V.M., and Dudley E. DeGroot, 1981.

Unwanted Pets and the Animal Shelter: The Pet Population Problem in New York State, Argus Archives report, 1973.

CHAPTER 3: "A Case of Cruelty"

ASPCA, New York; Denver Dumb Friends League; Humane Society of the United States, Washington, D.C.; Michigan Humane Society, Detroit.

CHAPTERS 4 AND 5: "Early Humane Societies"
and "Reformers and Defenders"

American Humane Education Society, Framingham Center, Mass.; Animal Rescue League of Boston; Anti-Cruelty Society, Chicago; Oregon Humane Society, Portland; Red Acre Farm, Stow, Mass.; Ryerss' Infirmary for Dumb Animals, Upper Darby, Pa.; Women's SPCA of Pennsylvania, Philadelphia.

Angel in Top Hat, by Zulma Steele.

"The Founder," by James Turner, *Animals* magazine (Mass. SPCA), Sept. and Oct. 1974.

Men, Beasts, and Gods: A History of Cruelty and Kindness to Animals, by Gerald Carson.

CHAPTER 6: "The Fight Against Dogfighting"

Arizona Humane Society, Phoenix; Humane Society of the United States, Washington, D.C.; Michigan Humane Society, Detroit.

Dogfighting in America: A National Overview, by Christopher Hoff, ASPCA, 1981.

"Pit!" by Craig M. Brown, *Atlanta* magazine, Feb. 1982.

CHAPTER 7: "Who Lives, Who Dies?"

ASPCA, New York; Denver Dumb Friends League; Humane Society of the United States, Washington, D.C.; the late Patty Jaymes of Animals Need You organization.

Bylaws and Policy Statements, the Atlanta Humane Society.

"Population Aspects of Animal Mortality," by Alan M. Beck, Sc.D., University of Pennsylvania, 1981.

CHAPTER 8: "Animal Control"

ASPCA, New York; Central Vermont Humane Society, Barre; Humane Society of New York; Humane Society of the United States, Washington, D.C.; Gretchen Scanlan, founder and former director, Kent Animal Shelter.

The NACA News. National Animal Control Association.

CHAPTER 9: "Pet Therapy Visits"

Animal Rescue League of Western Pennsylvania, Pittsburgh; Anti-Cruelty Society, Chicago; ASPCA, New York; Cleveland Animal Protective League; Dallas SPCA; Humane Society of Utah, Salt Lake City; Massachusetts SPCA, Boston; Oregon Humane Society, Portland; Pennsylvania SPCA, Philadelphia; San Diego County Humane Society and SPCA.

CHAPTER 10: "Humane Education"

ASPCA, New York; Atlanta Humane Society; Los Angeles SPCA; Gretchen Scanlan, founder and former director, Kent Animal Shelter; Wisconsin Humane Society, Milwaukee.

"Information on Selected Spay/Neuter Clinics and Programs," Humane Society of the United States, 1981.

CHAPTER 11: "Lost and Found"

Lawyers Committee for the Enforcement of Animal Protection Law, New York.

CHAPTER 12: "Wild Animal Pets"

Animal Protection Institute, Sacramento, Calif.; Unexpected Wildlife Refuge, Newfield, N.J.; Woodford Cedar Run Wildlife Refuge, Marlton, N.J.
"The Boa Next Door," by William Flanagan, *New York,* May 30, 1977.
"A House Is Not a Jungle," by Karen DeWitt, *The New York Times,* Nov. 22, 1980.
"Of Rabbits and Other Casualties of Easter," by Anna Quindlen, *The New York Times,* April 10, 1982.
"A Raccoon Can't Go Home Again," by Roger Caras, *Newsday,* Feb. 7, 1982.

CHAPTER 13: "Pets as Laboratory Tools"

ASPCA, New York; Fund for Animals, New York.
Alternatives to Pain in Experiments on Animals, by Dallas Pratt, M.D., Argus Archives, 1980.
"New Debate Over Experimenting with Animals," by Patricia Curtis, *The New York Times Magazine,* Dec. 31, 1978.
"Pound Seizure," *Animals* magazine (Mass. SPCA), April 1981.
"Protect Our Pets from Research," Humane Society of the United States, 1982.
"The Test Tube Alternative," by Andrew N. Rowan, *The Sciences,* Nov. 1981.

CHAPTER 14: "Adopted!"

Anti-Cruelty Society, Chicago; Pennsylvania SPCA, Philadelphia; Gretchen Scanlan, founder and former director, Kent Animal Shelter.

PAWS, newsletter of Progressive Animal Welfare Society, Lynnwood, Wash., Summer 1982.

Index

Page numbers in *italics* refer to captions.

About the Author
& Photographer

PATRICIA CURTIS is the author of many books and magazine articles about animals. Her books include *Animal Partners; Greff: The Story of a Guide Dog;* and *Cindy, A Hearing Ear Dog.*

"In this book, I am trying to speak for the pets that people have thrown away," she says. "I also hope to describe the wide range of work that shelter societies perform for animals and people alike."

Ms. Curtis lives in New York City with her dog and three cats—all pets that were unwanted by others. "Their loss was my gain," she emphasizes.

DAVID CUPP is a writer-photographer whose articles and pictures appear frequently in *National Geographic.* He and Patricia Curtis also collaborated on *Cindy, A Hearing Ear Dog.* He lives with his wife and four children in Denver, Colorado.